WAITING FOR *Christmas*

A HOT HOLIDAY ROMANCE

NEW YORK TIMES & *USA TODAY* BESTSELLING AUTHOR

CYNTHIA EDEN

DEDICATION

This one is for all the people who enjoy those romantic holiday movies...but wish they were a wee bit steamier. Ho, ho, ho.

CHAPTER ONE

When his doorbell rang after midnight, Wyatt Roth knew that trouble had to be on his doorstep. After all, a ringing doorbell in the middle of the night was never, ever a good sign. Just a basic fact of life. Wyatt stumbled toward the door, moving more like a zombie than anything else because his shift at the hospital had been long and brutal, and he'd just gotten to bed when—

The doorbell rang again. Louder. Longer. Or maybe it just seemed louder to him because his temples were already pounding.

He had one of those doorbell cameras installed, and the feed was going straight to his phone. Only the damn phone was hidden from him. Vaguely, Wyatt remembered putting the phone down to charge in the foyer. He wasn't on call with the hospital that night, so he'd left it downstairs and—

The doorbell rang again.

Anger stirred inside of him. Okay, some jackass had better *not* be playing. Wyatt wanted to yank the door open and give the jerk hell for waking him up. But caution held him back. He'd been trained to be cautious and to not take chances. So he grabbed his phone that was, indeed, charging on a table in the small foyer, he swiped his finger over the screen so he could see who the hell this late night visitor was, and...

Wyatt's breath left him in a rush. He dropped the phone back onto the table. Ran for the door and yanked it open in a flash. He yanked it open so quickly that the woman standing on the other side gave a startled scream and stumbled back in fear.

No way. You're not going anywhere. Wyatt's hand flew out and closed around her wrist. "Christy?" Wyatt said with both shock and delight. Shock because...*what the hell was she doing at his place?* And delight because—well, because the woman standing at his door, the woman who'd just woken him up after midnight— she was his obsession. His secret obsession from the time that he'd been fifteen years old.

Christmas "Christy" Sharpe stared back at him as the porch light shone down on her. Her brown eyes were shadowed, and she wore a red plaid coat that slid down to her thighs. Her long, dark hair tumbled over her shoulders. And beneath his hold? He could feel the frantic racing of her pulse.

Christy licked her lips. "Hi, um, Wyatt." Her gaze dropped down to his chest. And widened.

Because he wasn't wearing a shirt. Hell, he wasn't even wearing pants. Just his black boxers because he'd hauled ass out of bed when the doorbell kept pealing.

"I...woke you up. I'm sorry."

He shook his head. Of course, she'd woken him up. It was after midnight. But he wasn't shaking his head to deny her words. He was shaking his head because...*Is Christy really here? On my doorstep?* Or was he dreaming? Because he'd had this fantasy more than a few times. Only in his fantasy, she'd opened her coat to show that she wore nothing underneath it.

I can see her black pants. Clearly, she has clothes on beneath the coat. Unfortunately.

Christy shivered. "Can I come inside?" Her husky, slightly breathless voice rolled over Wyatt.

He hauled her in. Probably too desperately and eagerly. But when a dream appeared like a gift from the merry man in red, you held tightly to it. So he got her in, then he kicked the door shut and flipped the lock with his free hand...all while his right hand still gripped hers. He wasn't going to let her go. If he let her go, he'd probably wake up from what was promising to be one incredible dream.

Has to be a dream. Why the hell would Christy actually be at my door in the middle of the night? She barely spoke to him these days. And it had been around six months since he'd last seen her.

Dream. Definite dream. But, wow, was it vivid.

Her long, thick eyelashes flickered. "Um, thank you?" She bit her lip. "I know this is going to sound crazy, but can I spend the night with you?"

What. The. Hell? This dream felt incredibly, insanely real. Her pulse still raced beneath his touch, and he could have sworn that he smelled strawberries. Christy had worn strawberry body lotion for as long as he could remember. Usually, when he fantasized about her, he wasn't so aware of scents.

"Wyatt?" She shifted from one black booted foot to another. "Are you okay?" Her gaze darted down his body once more. A flush rose in her cheeks. "Oh, no. Did I interrupt something?" Her voice dropped to an embarrassed whisper. "Is someone else here with you?" Her stare flew toward the stairs. "Is there a woman up in your bedroom?"

Then, before he could speak, she yanked her hand free of his and tried to dart around him and get back to the door.

"Such a bad idea," she muttered. She fumbled with the lock. "I should never have come here. I'm so sorry. This is super embarrassing." She got the door open.

His hand slammed it closed.

In those few, frantic moments while Christy stammered her apology and tried to flee, Wyatt's sleep-fogged mind had finally managed to start processing properly, and he'd realized a few important points.

Point one. This was not one of his hot Christy dreams.

Point two. If it wasn't a dream, then Christy Sharpe was actually in his house. The real deal.

Point three. She wanted to spend the night with him.

Point four? He was fucking things up, and she was running away.

"No one else is here," he said, aware that his voice came out as little more than a growl. Wyatt cleared his throat and tried again. "It's just us."

She turned around.

He didn't move back, so when she turned, Christy wound up being trapped between his body and the door that he'd just shut so forcefully. His hand remained up and pressed to the wood of that door, and he was leaning toward her. Even in those high boots of hers, Christy was still a few inches shorter than he was. She'd always been on the delicate side.

He'd always wanted to protect her.

She'd always...

Thought I was just the kid who hung around with her little brother. Because he had, in fact, always been best friends with Christy's younger brother, Forth. Wyatt and Forth had been inseparable as kids. Were still tight as adults. And the fact that Wyatt had been mooning over Forth's sister for freaking years?

Well, that was intel that Forth didn't need to know.

Wyatt stared into Christy's eyes. Flecks of gold were buried in the heart of her dark eyes. Her skin was flushed—from embarrassment?—and her lips had been painted a slick red. He found himself staring a little too hard at her lips, so he whipped his gaze upward. "Why are you here?"

The question was torn from him. "I didn't even know you were coming home."

Home. Birmingham, Alabama. Or, more specifically, a tiny little slice just outside of Birmingham...Mountain Brook.

"Did you get bigger?" Christy blurted.

He blinked.

Her rosy flush grew darker. "That is not what I intended to say. I meant to say—you're naked."

He blinked once more.

"No." Her eyes squeezed shut. "Not naked. Mostly naked. You're mostly naked and...do you want to put on clothes?"

Not particularly, he didn't. He'd rather get her *out* of her clothes. "Christy." Wyatt waited for her eyes to flutter open. When they did... "Why were you standing on my doorstep at this time of night?"

Her white teeth lightly pressed to her plump, lower lip.

Oh, but how he would love to be biting that lip. Wyatt made sure to keep his lower body away from her. If she looked down that far, though, all bets were going to be very, very off. There would be no missing the giant erection thrusting toward her.

"Can I stay with you?" Christy whispered. "I know it is a terrible inconvenience for me to show up out of the blue—"

"Always," he cut in to say.

A furrow appeared between her brows. Shit. Wyatt ran back through the words they'd both just spoken. It probably sounded like he'd meant her showing up was always a terrible inconvenience.

That hadn't been his intention. He *did* always get stupid nervous around her, and he basically reverted to being an unsure teen. Dammit. That shit had to stop. "You can *always* stay with me," he corrected forcefully. He inhaled. Wow. She smelled freaking delicious. Good enough to eat.

I wish.

"Forth isn't in town," Christy said.

Right. "He's in Paris. Won't be back for another week."

Her chin lifted. "I didn't know that. I-I didn't call him before I came home. I actually just packed my bags and hopped in my car and drove as fast as I could to get here. I needed somewhere safe to crash, so I thought I'd come to Mountain Brook."

Home. To Christy, home would mean the house she grew up in. The house her brother Forth now owned. Her parents had died when Christy was twenty-one and Forth had been twenty. Since then, she'd rarely come back to Mountain Brook. Mostly just for visits with Forth during the holidays.

No, not true. She also came home when I lost my parents. Christy helped me. Comforted me. Made sure I wasn't alone.

But then she'd left. He'd graduated college. Med school. Christy had focused on her art. She'd opened a glassblowing studio in Asheville, North Carolina. Hell, he and Forth had helped her paint the place before the big opening. He'd wanted her to be happy, wherever she was.

Sometimes, he thought *home* held too many painful memories for her. The night of her parents' accident had changed everything for Christy, he knew that. That night had sure scared the fuck out of him.

Because she was in the car. And at first, we all thought we'd lose her, too. Did she even get that he was a doctor because of her? Because he'd been so fucking grateful to the surgeons who'd saved her?

But home had become hard and scary for Christy after that. Because the parents she'd loved so dearly had been gone.

But she'd just called her old home *safe,* and that one word pierced straight through him because...why would Christy need a safe place? Every muscle in his body suddenly tensed as he went on high alert. "What's wrong?"

She grimaced. "Someone is obsessed with me."

Hell. She knows. He shot away from the door. Away from her. Spun so that his back was to her. How had she found out the truth? And, really, wasn't *obsessed* a strong word? Not like he was a full-on stalker. "Look, I can explain—"

"I made a mistake. Got involved with someone that I shouldn't have."

His mouth clamped shut. His spine also stiffened even more.

"I have a dangerous ex. He won't let go." Christy's words tumbled out in a fearful rush.

Wyatt whirled back to face her.

"He broke into my house. Destroyed some of my things. And I was—I needed to come someplace where I would be safe." Her hands twisted in front of her. "I thought I'd go to Forth, but he was gone." Her head shook. "I should have called him first. I was just panicked and not thinking clearly. I got in the car and drove. Fleeing was my first instinct. Then when Forth wasn't home, I-I couldn't stay there alone. The house was so big and dark." Her gaze had dipped to the floor, but it suddenly rose to pin his. "I should have called you, too. Instead of just showing up here. But my instinct was just to run to you. I knew exactly how to get to your house because I helped you move in last June, remember?"

Like he'd ever been able to forget a single thing about her. *My instinct was just to run to you.* Hell, yes, that should be her instinct. She could always run to him. Always.

"May I please just stay here for the night?"

She was begging him? "No."

She backed up. Her elbow rammed into the door.

Dammit. He'd done it again. *Say things clearly to her.* He marched toward her. "You're not staying for the night. You're staying here with me until Forth comes back. And you are going to tell me *everything* about this sonofabitch who is scaring you." *So that I can utterly destroy him.* Because Christy had never been the type to scare easily. She was bold and wild. The life of the party. One of those people who literally lit up a room when she was in it.

Or, at least, she'd always lit up rooms for him.

She wasn't uncertain. Wasn't scared. Wasn't the type to tremble with fear. Yet she was trembling right now. All he wanted to do was pull her into his arms. Hold her tight. And promise her that he would never, ever let anything bad happen to her.

Wyatt caught his arms actually lifting to embrace her.

Whoa. Slow down there, jackass. The woman is terrified. Now wasn't the time to be working his own agenda. He needed to focus on eliminating all threats to her.

A slow smile spread as her lips curved. Relief lit her dark eyes. "Really? You'll be okay with me staying? I swear, I-I will try not to be any trouble."

She had no idea that she'd always been trouble for him. "I am definitely okay with you staying." *You can stay in my bed, if you want. The better for me to keep you safe and to fuck you all night long.* He growled. Nope. That would be the wrong thing to say. "I have a guest room." One that was located right next to his on the second floor. "You can stay there."

That smile of hers got even bigger and flashed the dimple in her right cheek. Just one dimple. So damn adorable.

"Thank you!" Christy beamed. Then, before he realized what he was going to do, Christy hurled herself into his arms and hugged him fiercely.

And by *hurled*...she pressed herself tightly against every single inch of his body. Or at least, all the inches she could touch. When she stiffened and gasped, he knew she had absolutely not missed the giant hard-on thrusting toward her.

Her head snapped back, and she stared at him with wide eyes. "I—" Christy stopped. Cleared her throat.

Yeah, sure, they could try ignoring his dick. *Good luck with that.*

"I must have...ah, woken you up in the middle of an intense dream," she mumbled.

Really? She was making excuses for him? Hey, at least she wasn't ignoring the situation.

She pulled back. "You're a doctor. I'm sure you know all about random, physiological reactions."

Wyatt crossed his arms over his chest.

Christy was looking everywhere but at him. And by everywhere...well, now she was focusing on the Christmas tree in his den. The one that had lights but no ornaments.

"You've decorated!" A too bright note had entered her voice. "It looks great!"

The tree did not, in fact, look great. Zero ornaments. Zero presents. Just some lights. "It's not random." Why had he said that? Why not just let this go?

Her gaze flew back to him.

And he knew that he was *done* letting things go where she was concerned. *Some sonofabitch terrified her. She ran to me. That means I get to stop pretending.*

"Excuse me?" Christy's voice notched up.

"The hard-on?"

She blushed again. God, he loved her blush.

"I know it's nothing personal—" she began.

"It is extremely personal. It's all about you. Just so we are clear."

Her mouth dropped open.

How fun would it be to thrust his tongue past those parted lips of hers? *Not yet. Not. Yet.* "I've wanted you for years. But I'm not some psycho asshole who is going to take advantage when you're scared. I can control myself. Always have. Always will." She needed to understand this. "You have nothing to ever fear from me."

"You've...wanted—what?" Her words ended in a little squeak.

Oh, yes. He was one hundred percent oversharing. And if it hadn't been helluva-late-o'thirty, he would have shut his fool mouth. But, nope, he just opened it and said, quite clearly, "I've wanted you for years. Since you were sixteen, to be exact." The summer she'd first worked as a lifeguard at the country club's pool.

And he'd thought about faking a drowning just so she could give him mouth-to-mouth.

"But, you're...you're Forth's best friend—"

"Absolutely. Would die for him in an instant." *But I would also gladly die—or kill—to protect you.*

"You're my little brother's—"

His hands fell to his sides. Deliberately, he closed in on her. She retreated, backing toward the den. Toward the tree with the lights that gleamed softly. "I'm not so little any longer."

She had run out of room to retreat. The tree waited behind her. He'd put the tree up yesterday. Even though it was just him for the holidays, he'd needed it up because the place had just felt too cold and empty.

With Christy there, it didn't feel cold at all. Nothing ever felt cold when she was near. Especially not him. When she was close, he felt burning hot.

"Christy, I stopped being little a long time ago."

And, holy hell, her gaze dropped down his body.

Is she looking at my dick? Sure seemed that way to him.

Her stare jumped right back up. "I can see that. Definitely not little." She squeezed her eyes shut. "Why did I just say that?"

She was so cute.

"I drove for five and a half hours to get here from Asheville. I was scared to death the entire time. I am not in control." A slow exhale of breath as her eyes opened. "I am not in control," she told him again.

"Don't worry, I am." And he wasn't going to do anything she didn't want. Not ever. "Let's get you to bed. We can talk in the morning." She looked absolutely delectable with the tree lights behind her, but he still turned away. Acted like it was the easiest thing in the world when turning away from Christy would never be easy. "And by talk," he added over his shoulder, "I mean you are going to tell me everything about the bastard who is terrorizing you. Then I'm going to pull some strings, and we will make sure that he never, ever so much as looks at you sideways again."

Silence from behind him.

He continued toward the stairs. When he didn't hear her boots clicking on the floor as she followed him, Wyatt finally looked back.

"Who are you?" Christy asked as if he was a stranger and not someone she'd known most of her life.

"I'm the man you need right now." A shrug. *I've always been him. But maybe you'll finally see me now.*

"You're a doctor. You don't—you don't deal with—"

"I'm SOST." Not just a doctor. He went into the battlefield whenever he and his team were needed. "Special Operations Surgical Team." He turned to fully face her. "I've supported Special Operations Forces all over the world. I've been in every high stress situation you can imagine—and plenty I hope you never, ever have to imagine. This asshole scaring you? He's made a fatal mistake. No one should scare you. I'll take care of him. Consider this *done.*"

She stumbled toward him. Usually, she was all grace. Practically ballerina-like with her movements. Her stumble told him more than words ever could. Christy was near the end of her rope.

There is more going on here than she's revealed. But, come morning, he would get her to reveal every secret to him.

"When did you grow up?" Christy breathed.

"When you weren't looking." She was almost in front of him. All he wanted was to scoop her into his arms and—

Screw it. He did.

A gasp broke from her when he lifted her up against his chest. He put one arm under her knees and the other braced behind her back.

Christy automatically curled her arm around his neck. "What are you doing?"

"Carrying you up the stairs." That should be pretty obvious.

"But...I can walk."

"You can. I can also carry you." She was too light. She'd lost weight since June. *Because of the man scaring her?* Just how long had she been afraid and on her own? That shit was over. "You're dead on your feet. Driving when you're exhausted is dangerous. Driving at night when you're exhausted? Even more so." A reminder she shouldn't need, not with her parents.

She flinched, and he hated that he'd just caused her pain.

"I stayed alert. Stopped at rest areas. Walked around."

She'd walked around dark rest areas by herself? Fantastic. He growled.

"You keep making these angry little sounds," she murmured. "Wyatt, are you mad at me?"

No, sweetheart, I just want to fucking eat you alive. "Lost a patient today," he said. A grim truth. He'd fought like hell, but in the end, there had been no saving the sixteen-year-old gunshot victim. "I'm not at my best."

"Oh, Wyatt, I'm so sorry." She held him tighter. And...wait, had she just pressed a kiss to his cheek? She had. Not a kiss of passion. But of comfort.

His body reacted as if it had been passion, though.

His dick had a hard time interpreting things clearly. *Hard time. Hah. I'm fucking hilarious.*

"Do you want to talk about it?" she asked softly.

"Not tonight." Tonight, he needed to push the memory away. He always had to push the memories down deep. But they'd trickle out later. Come at him in flashes when he'd wish he could have done something more.

Focus on what is right in front of you. That was his motto. And what was right in front of him?

Christy.

At the top of the stairs, he turned to the right. Went past his room and into the guest room. "Turn on the light," he ordered her.

She reached out and flipped the switch.

He carried her to the bed. Lowered her slowly. Forced himself to let go and step back.

"My...my luggage is in the car." A wince. "I should have mentioned that before you carried me upstairs."

"I'll get it. You stay here." He took her car keys and backed away from the bed. One step. Another.

Then he double-timed it down the stairs. When he searched her Jeep, he was surprised to just find one bag. Christy was never the type to travel light. *Loaded down* was way more her style. Wyatt headed back inside and paused to make sure the alarm was set. When he was certain that the house was secure, only then did he go back up the stairs.

When he entered the guest room, she'd ditched her coat. She stood beside the bed. No coat. No boots. A whole lot shorter.

Unlike in his fantasies, she wasn't naked.

He dropped the luggage on the floor. "The bathroom is through that door." He pointed to the right. "I've got plenty of shampoo and conditioner in there. Use whatever you need." A swallow. "I'm in the bedroom beside you, so if you should need me for anything..." *Anything at all.* "You come get me. Or just shout. I'll hear you and come running." Always.

A jerky nod. Her arms wrapped around her waist. "Thank you. I am really grateful—"

"Don't want your gratitude."

"What do you want?"

He knew his mask cracked. She sucked in a quick breath, and Wyatt understood that she'd just glimpsed the hunger he normally held in careful check for her. But it was late, it had been a bitch of a day, and he wasn't his normal self. Wyatt turned for the door. "Good night, Christy."

"You don't...Wyatt, you want me? Really?"

His fingers flew up and grabbed the doorframe.

"You never said a word about wanting me. If you've wanted me since I was sixteen, why didn't you say something sooner?"

He nearly ripped off that doorframe. "If I'd told you back then, when we were teens, what would you have said?"

"You...you're my little brother's best friend."

And you are the star of my fantasies. Then and now. "That's what you would have said when you were sixteen. You're not sixteen any longer."

"Wyatt, I—"

"You're scared and you're running on fumes. Get some sleep, Christy." He exhaled slowly. "You're safe. And I'm right next door." He walked out and closed the door softly behind him.

***

Click.

Christy didn't move. She couldn't move. Shock held her immobile. "Why didn't you say something sooner, Wyatt?" she whispered.

So much sooner.

CHAPTER TWO

Surely, he wouldn't be as hot first thing in the morning.

Christy slowly opened the guest room door. Just a wee little crack. Enough for her to peek out into the hallway.

No sign of Wyatt.

No way—no way—would he be as hot. She'd been half delirious the previous night. So...so he'd maybe looked like some awesome Greek god come to life. With a crazy six pack, with shoulders that would make a linebacker jealous, and the sexiest, thickest tousled hair that she'd ever seen. As always, his blue gaze had been positively electric. But that stare of his...

It had seemed *different*. No, there had been something different *in* it when he looked at her and—

And he'd been turned on.

She'd been terrified. Not of him—never of Wyatt—and she'd had the absolutely crazy urge to throw herself against him and hold on tight. And when she'd done that throwing, there had been no missing the obvious, um, physical response he'd had.

And I thought about that response for far too long before finally drifting to sleep.

The best sleep she'd had in weeks. Because—hopefully, finally—she was safe.

She cracked the door open a little bit more. No sign of Wyatt. She sprinted out and down the stairs. It was barely six a.m. He had to still be sleeping. She'd grab some coffee, come up with a plan, and be ready to get out of his hair, ASAP. Because as her fear had retreated, Christy had realized that she could not just move in with Wyatt for the holidays.

She'd be fine at Forth's house. The previous night, she'd let fear get the best of her. But she was far from Asheville now. She was *safe*.

Her bare feet flew down the stairs, and she zipped toward his kitchen. A big, white, swinging door separated his den from the kitchen. She shoved it open as she hurried inside to—"Ah!" A scream tore from her.

Wyatt winced. He also kept lounging against the counter and sipping what looked like a steaming mug of coffee. "Good morning to you, too, sunshine."

Her hand had automatically moved to cover her racing heart. She was so jumpy these days. *That is what happens when you have a creep watching your every move. Slipping into your gallery. Breaking into your house.* "I thought you were sleeping."

"No. I woke up early for my usual five-mile run, but then realized I couldn't leave you unprotected."

Her brows rose. "Usual five-mile run?" People did that as a usual thing? Like, a daily thing? Without being chased? Of their own free will? How interesting. And also... "Unprotected?"

"You might have woken up alone and been scared. Couldn't have that."

She rocked back on her heels. Mostly because the casual care in his words just took her breath away. He hadn't wanted her to be scared. Other than her brother, Wyatt was probably the only person she knew who would care if she was scared.

"I'll get you some coffee." He put down his mug and turned toward his rather fancy machine setup.

Christy took that moment to admire his broad back and the sheer power of his build. He wore black sweatpants. Running shoes. No shirt. He seemed to have some sort of issue with shirts. First, he had been shirtless last night, and now this morning. And—

"Here you go." He'd turned toward her and extended a mug.

She took it. Her fingers brushed his, and she did not imagine the electric charge that went through her at the touch. Just as she hadn't imagined the same charge last night, when he'd scooped her into his arms and carried her up the stairs like that was a normal thing. Talk about being strong and fierce.

She hadn't imagined the attraction she felt for him. An attraction that had hit her randomly a few times over the years. But she'd ignored it because...

Forth's best friend. She could not have a fling with her little brother's best friend. No way.

Right?

She already had enough trouble in her life, thank you very much. And getting involved with the very hot doctor standing before her? *Lots and lots of trouble.* "I need to add some cream and a bit of sugar," she murmured. "Mind if I—"

"Already added it for you." His hand pulled away. He returned to leaning casually against the counter, and his electric eyes locked on her. "I know how you like your coffee, Christy."

She sipped the coffee. Holy crap, he did know how she liked it. The coffee was one hundred percent perfect.

"I know how you like your coffee. I know your favorite color. Red, by the way. That's why you have so much red in your wardrobe. I know your favorite song. Your favorite movie—it's *The Mummy*. The one with Brendan Fraser. I know your favorite hiking trail. I know your favorite holiday. Spoiler alert, it's not Christmas. It's actually Halloween. Probably because it always drove you a little crazy that your parents named you Christmas. But you were born on Christmas Eve, so..."

So you know a whole lot about me. She took another quick, invigorating sip of the coffee. "Christmas for me, and they named my brother Forth because he was born on the Fourth of July."

Though they had at least spelled Forth's name differently. *Mom and Dad, I miss you so much.* Her family had been so happy when she'd been growing up. Everything had been perfect.

Until it wasn't.

Until her parents were gone. Until she'd woken in a hospital hooked to so many tubes. Forth had been on one side of her. Wyatt on the other. They'd told her she wasn't alone.

Then...Forth had gone back to MIT. Wyatt had been busy planning for his career in medicine. She'd tried to start fresh in Asheville. Things had worked out, at first.

Until they hadn't.

Until she'd been lost and alone and scared and...

And I came running home.

Wyatt kept watching her. "I thought I knew everything about you..."

No, not everything.

"Except I didn't know the fact that you had some sonofabitch stalking you. *Why* didn't I know that, Christy?"

She swallowed. "It's a recent situation—"

"Define recent."

She flinched because this was gonna be bad. "Three months."

He shot away from the counter. For a moment, she thought he was lunging at her, but he caught himself. His hands jerked back and locked around the counter. He used that locking grip to haul himself back into place. "Three months."

A nod.

"Three fucking months."

Another nod.

"Does Forth know?"

Her lips parted.

"Of course, he doesn't know," Wyatt fired before she could answer. "He would have told me. He would have never left the freaking country if he'd thought some jerk was stalking you. You kept this secret from both of us."

Yes, she had. "I was trying to handle things on my own." She'd just wanted it all to stop. Only instead of stopping, things had gotten much, much worse.

"So you fucked a guy, and he couldn't let go. Bastard went off the deep end and now he's—"

The mug slipped from her fingers. It shouldn't have, but it did. And it seemed to tumble toward the floor in slow motion. Automatically, she jerked backward, fearful of the hot coffee splashing back at her. The mug hit the tiled floor, it shattered, and chunks of glass and coffee flew everywhere.

"Christy!" Wyatt jumped toward her. His hands locked around her waist. He lifted her up, carried her over the broken shards and spilled coffee, and sat her on top of the counter. "Baby, where are you hurt?"

"I—"

His hands flew over her. She wore loose pajama pants and a tank top. She *hadn't* thought he'd be up so early, so Christy hadn't changed before coming downstairs. Her mistake. He caught the bottom of her pants and pushed them up, searching her calves and bare feet for any injuries.

"I didn't fuck him," Christy heard herself say.

His hold tightened on her left calf. "You're not burned."

She shook her head.

His blue stare lifted to meet hers. "You didn't fuck him." He let go of her calf. But Wyatt didn't back away. Big, strong, *grown-up* Wyatt pressed his hands down against the counter on either side of her body. Heat and power seemed to swirl around him. A dark shadow of stubble covered his hard jaw, and his thick hair was even more tousled than it had been the night before.

Stop focusing on his hair and stubble. "W-we just went out a few times. Things never got that far."

His blue eyes narrowed. "Are you telling me what you think I want to hear?"

She squinted at him. "Why would I do that?" Why would she ever run screaming from him?

"Because I'm a jealous asshole, and I don't want you fucking anyone but me."

Her eyes had to be huge. She could *feel* them widening. He was...jealous? And he didn't want her fucking...oh, wow.

This was not what she'd expected at all. "Would you say that again?"

"Sorry," he bit out instead. "Not what you need to hear right now. Dammit, I swore that I would be supportive and *cool* this morning. But here I am, probably about to send you running from me, screaming."

She'd actually gone running *to* him the night before. Christy couldn't ever remember a time that she'd actually run from Wyatt. Wyatt was her safe place. So it was her turn to ask once more, "Why would I do that?"

His jaw tightened. "This isn't the time to play with me."

Did it look as if she was playing?

"Don't move, okay?" His voice had gone extra gruff. "I'm cleaning up the mess. Your feet are bare, and the last thing I want is for you to get cut."

"I—"

He was already cleaning up the glass. Tossing the bigger chunks in the trash. Wiping up the spilled coffee. Sweeping the smaller shards into a dustpan. A fast. efficient clean, and then he was back in front of her. "Good as new," he murmured.

"I'm sorry about the mug."

"Fuck it. I don't care about it." His stare held hers. "I care about you."

She didn't just hear those words. She could practically *feel* them pouring over her.

"I barely got any sleep last night. Kept thinking about some prick trying to hurt you. About you being scared and on your own and not coming to me for help. Drove myself crazy. I walked by your bedroom door at least three times just to make sure I didn't hear you crying out from a bad dream or something."

He had?

"What if he'd followed you?" Wyatt demanded. "That's a long drive from Asheville to

Mountain Brook. Lots of twisting roads. What if he'd caught you? What if he'd forced you off the road? What if—"

Her right hand rose and pressed to his chest. "I don't like 'what if' talk."

His lashes flickered.

She was touching his bare skin. Warm. Muscled. Wyatt. "I've found that just spinning around with 'what if' scenarios will make you crazy. Better to just deal with the present. With what is right in front of you." And Wyatt was right in front of her.

A Wyatt who seemed so incredibly different from the boy—the man—she'd known for so long.

His nostrils flared. "I want his name."

"Jesse Mitchell. He owns two night clubs in Asheville. I-I met him when he came to my studio and commissioned me to do some glass work for him." She'd been so excited by the opportunity. Christy swallowed. "After I finished the commissioned work, we went out two or three times. But something just felt...off."

"Off how?"

This was where she wasn't going to be able to explain. Because so often, none of her dates felt...*right*. And it was probably crazy, but she just wanted... "The spark wasn't there. The connection you're supposed to feel." The wild connection that she was feeling for Wyatt right then and there. Another quick swallow. "I felt nervous with him. Like, I'd catch him watching me, and I swear, he would look...angry."

"You broke it off with him." Not a question.

"After the third date, I told him that it wasn't working. I honestly thought he felt the same way and then..." Her voice trailed away. She started to lift her hand away from Wyatt because Christy had just realized she'd still been touching him. No, caressing him.

But his hand flew up and locked around her wrist, holding her in place. "Then what happened, Christy?"

"My glass was broken," she whispered and had to blink away tears. She'd poured her heart and soul into her glassblowing studio. "I walked in and everything there—all the work I'd done for the last month—it had been shattered. The floor was covered in shards of glass."

"Sonofabitch."

"I-I didn't know that it was him."

"You have a security system at the studio. Forth and I helped you install it—"

"Someone took my cameras offline. When I spoke to the cops, I didn't have any evidence to give them showing the culprit. One of the detectives wanted to know about people in my life who might be angry with me, and that's...that's when I mentioned Jesse." A slow exhale. "The detective's expression changed. I *saw* the flash of alarm, but he didn't say anything to me, not then." But she'd felt Detective Warren Langston's concern. "He waited until the other officers had left, then Detective Langston whispered to me that I needed to be on my guard around Jesse. He told me that the department was investigating him. That Jesse had criminal ties. That he should be considered very dangerous."

Wyatt's fingers slid along her wrist.

"That night, when I went home, a dozen roses were waiting for me. A note was with them. A note that said, 'Without you, I'll be as broken as your glass.'" She shivered. "The roses were *inside* my condo. He'd gotten in, and it scared the hell out of me. I called him. Told him to stay away from me."

Wyatt's features tightened into a mask of fury. "But he didn't."

"I could feel someone watching me. I changed my locks at the studio and at my condo. Got new security cameras installed. But they were taken out again. And...the reason I ran last night..." *Tell him.* "When I got home, my place was trashed. Pictures broken, my glass pieces that I kept in my display case—they were shattered. And there was another note."

"What did it say?" Flat.

Her lips trembled, so she pressed them together.

"Christy..."

"It said, 'This time, you'll be the one who is broken.'"

"He's a dead man." He jerked from her and whirled away.

"No!" Christy jumped off the counter and grabbed his arm. "I left him behind. He's not going to come here. He won't. I'm safe."

Wyatt turned to stare down at her. His eyes glittered.

"I'm safe with you...right?" she asked as her hold tightened on him.

He caught her hand. Brought it to his mouth. Pressed a soft kiss to her knuckles. "Always."

A shiver slid over her. One that had nothing to do with fear. And everything to do with Wyatt. "He won't know about you. He won't know that I'm here."

"You need a restraining order."

Her head shook. "Couldn't get one. I didn't have any proof to link him to the attacks. He denied everything when the cops questioned him."

"We'll get proof."

He acted like it would be easy. Nothing had been easy for the last few months. "I'm tired of being scared," she murmured. "I want to stop looking over my shoulder. I just want to feel normal for a while." She wasn't even asking to feel happy again. Just normal. Christy was so tired of being on edge and always looking over her shoulder.

It was the holiday season. The most magical time of the year, right? At least, that was what her parents used to say. She'd come home because she could sure use a little of that Christmas magic.

Wyatt's head moved in a determined nod. "I have connections. Friends who will help. We're getting proof. We're stopping him." His hand rose to cup her jaw. "You believe me? You hear what I'm telling you? We will stop him."

Her heart slammed into her chest. She wanted to believe him. But the cops in Asheville had been tracking Jesse for ages, and they still couldn't pin him to anything. So everyone else in the area just went right on thinking he was some upstanding businessman.

Only he's not. He terrifies me.

"Christy, you're staying with me until we catch him."

"Uh..." *Catching* him could be something that took a lot of time. "Maybe he'll forget me now that I've left town. Maybe he will—"

Wyatt shook his head. "Guys like him don't forget. I've seen the damage those freak stalkers can do. I've had their vics on my table. That will *not* happen to you."

Now her heart wasn't just pounding. Her stomach was knotting. Her breath almost panting.

"You are safe," he told her flatly. "I have you."

The moment was too tense. Too emotional. Too everything. She pulled away, and his hand fell back to his side. She forced down the lump in her throat and tried to tease, "The kid who used to chase me in tag is gonna protect me now?"

"Stop." An order. A growl.

Her arms wrapped around her stomach.

"First, I always caught you in tag. Always."

Yes, actually, he had. Wyatt had been damn fast.

"Second, I stopped being a kid a long time ago."

She could see that.

"And I've seen things—done things—that would give you nightmares."

Her brows flew up. Now he was the one keeping secrets—

"I can handle bastards like him," Wyatt assured her in a dark and dangerous tone. "Don't you worry. You will be safe." A vow.

A vow she believed.

"I want to get moving on this. First order of business—I want to see your phone. I want to see any texts he sent you."

Her phone. Right. She winced. "I think I left it in my car." She'd been running for the front door pretty fast last night. Jumping at shadows. "And weren't you about to go for a jog?" She didn't want to stop him from doing his normal routine.

"Fuck the jog. I'm taking care of you." A decisive nod. "I'll get the phone." He snagged her keys from the counter. She hadn't even noticed them. Christy figured he must have dropped them on the counter sometime after he'd brought in her luggage.

He was already making his way through the den, so she hurried after him. Wyatt shoved open the front door and rushed down the porch steps. Her bare feet curled over the cold wood of the porch. It was a brisk morning, and a faint frost covered all of the lawns on the well-to-do cul-de-sac.

"*Don't move.*"

Wyatt's sharp warning stopped her just as Christy was climbing down the steps. Her head whipped up.

"I think we can assume you *were* followed."

The chill from the early frost was nothing compared to the ice that suddenly covered her. Because she could clearly see her Jeep from her perch on the steps. See the Jeep...

And see that her Jeep sat...oddly in the driveway. Oddly as in...

All four tires are completely flat.

Wyatt crouched near the front, right tire. "Slashed," he gritted out before shoving upright. He whirled toward her. "The sonofabitch followed you last night. He had a knife with him. He took out all of your tires." He ran back to her and jumped up the steps. With careful hands, Wyatt urged her back inside the house before slamming and locking the door. "The bastard was *here*," he rasped as his hands curled around her shoulders.

She couldn't speak. *He followed me? All during that long, twisting drive?*

"If you'd stayed at Forth's place alone..." A shudder went over him. One that sure looked like a shudder of fury. "He could have tried to break in. Gotten *you*."

Chills raced up and down her body.

"You will not be alone. You will not be out of my sight, understand?" Wyatt pulled her closer. She could feel the faint calluses on his fingertips. "No one will hurt you, I swear it."

But she shivered because...

Christy had just realized that, in fleeing, she hadn't escaped her danger.

She'd just brought it home with her.

CHAPTER THREE

A Christmas party.

Wyatt glanced around the brightly decorated staff room, and his gaze locked right on Christy. She was smiling and nodding and seeming a bit more relaxed than she'd been earlier in the day...

When they had to talk to the freaking cops because her psycho stalker had followed her to town.

The bastard was at my house. He could have even been watching when Wyatt had gone back out for Christy's luggage. The jerk had been right there, armed with a knife. *He could have used that knife on Christy.* Like that wouldn't give Wyatt nightmares for the rest of his life.

Wyatt's gaze remained on Christy. He wanted her within sight at all times, and if he could have, they would have skipped the damn Christmas party.

But...

She'd been the one to insist that they attend. Once she'd realized that it was a charity event where the staff would be bringing in presents for the kids at the hospital, she'd insisted they come. And maybe it had been good to get out of the house. To take her to a place where she could relax. Mix and mingle with some other people. Celebrate the holidays a bit.

So, even though Wyatt would have preferred to whisk her far away and lock Christy in the most secretive, secure place imaginable...

They were currently at the hospital Christmas party. All of the donated toys were in a giant pile beneath the tree. A tree that had been decorated with paper chains—courtesy of the kids in the pediatric wing—and with hand-painted angels—those from the "Angel" volunteer staff members who came to stay so often with the NICU babies.

"So that's the infamous Christy Sharpe." A man in green scrubs came to stand beside Wyatt. "I can definitely see the attraction. No wonder you've been hooked on her for years." A low whistle slid from him. "Very, very nice."

"Don't even think it, Axel," he warned his buddy as Wyatt did not take his gaze from Christy. "Erase the thought. Never have it. Bury it in a deep, dark pit."

Axel Bishop laughed. "Red looks good on her."

She wore a red sweater. Black pants. Her killer boots. And she was helping arrange the presents that would be donated. Her smile was quick and easy, and her dimple flashed whenever she laughed. Anyone looking at her—and, unfortunately, plenty of guys were eyeing her—

would think she probably didn't have a care in the world.

They'd have no idea she'd cried in his den that morning when the cops came to his house. The jerk who'd sliced her tires had stayed out of the range of his security cameras. *Smart bastard.* She'd cried, and all Wyatt had wanted to do was put his fist through a wall.

Or through Jesse Mitchell's face.

"Everything looks good on her," Wyatt returned in response to Axel's words. He tried to keep his tone at least partially civil. After all, he liked Axel. They were on the same special ops surgical team. They'd trained together. Worked together. Seen hell together.

But the guy really needed to stop drinking in Christy.

"You talk with Finn yet?" Axel asked him.

Finn O'Connor. Not part of SOST. Not technically, anyway, though he certainly hung plenty with the team. While Axel and Wyatt were doctors, Finn was more of...well, a straight-up nightmare for the enemy. A former SEAL turned detective, Wyatt and Axel had needed to sew Finn back together on a battlefield one horribly bloody time.

Finn had never let them forget that he owed them a debt. At least, a debt in his mind.

When Finn had left the service, he'd hung out a shingle for his own PI-slash-security business. And, yep, Wyatt had definitely talked with Finn about the mess going down. "Called him as soon as the cops left my house. He's digging on Jesse Mitchell now."

Axel grunted.

Wyatt had also briefed Axel before arriving at the party, mostly because he wanted another person on guard while he had Christy at the hospital. Every moment, Wyatt felt on edge. He worried another attack might come at any time. "The bastard was right outside my house, and I didn't know it."

"I'm sure you were busy with..." Axel cleared his throat. "Other things last night."

Wyatt finally looked away from Christy. He turned and stepped in front of his friend. "Watch it."

Axel's head tilted to the left. "Does Forth know that she's sleeping with you?"

"Sleeping at my *house*." Oh, but what he wouldn't give to sleep with her. "And, no, we haven't talked to him yet. Tried calling but just got his voicemail. You know how hard international calls can be sometimes."

"But you *are* going to tell him?" Axel pushed.

"Tell him that some sick prick is stalking his sister? Yeah, he deserves to know that." And Wyatt had to glance over his shoulder to look at her.

Still safe. Still smiling. Still tying bows with careful precision on the gifts that will be donated.

In that moment, Christy turned her head and caught sight of Wyatt. Or rather, she caught him staring at her.

A light blush rose in her cheeks, and her smile widened.

His breath shuddered out.

"Aw, jeez, man." Axel had moved to his side. Probably so he could get a better view of Christy. The dick. "You are so freaking transparent," Axel continued with a sigh. "Was it always this bad? Or did you suddenly get much, much worse when she slept-in-your-house-but-not-with-you   last night?"

"I will kick your ass," Wyatt told Axel pleasantly. "And lower the volume of your voice, now."

"Uh, huh. Lowering it." And he did. "But have you thought about how much Forth is gonna want to kick *your* ass? Because something tells me you aren't going to be letting her sleep alone much longer. Especially not with the way you just looked at her...and she just looked at you."

"I can handle Forth."

"You didn't deny the part about letting her sleep alone..."

No, he hadn't.

Because if he had his way, Wyatt would be sleeping with her as soon as possible.

***

"So you're the one."

Christy tied the last bow in place and glanced toward the nurse who'd just made that announcement. "The one?" she inquired carefully.

Naya Yale nodded. She'd introduced herself right after Christy had arrived at the party. Her dark eyes were curious as they slid over Christy's face. "The one who finally landed our hot doc."

Hot doc. Instantly, her gaze flew to Wyatt.

And she found him staring back at her with an undeniably predatory, almost…hungry expression in his brilliant blue eyes. Christy felt the flush rising in her cheeks as she tried to hold his stare.

"When you walked through the hospital doors with him tonight, I recognized you instantly," Naya said, sounding rather pleased with herself.

Christy forced her gaze off Wyatt and onto Naya. "Recognized me? How?" She'd never been to a hospital event before with Wyatt.

"Dr. Roth has an office upstairs. Your picture is on his desk." Naya smiled at her. Her black hair curled lightly around her heart-shaped face. "Always a dead giveaway when a guy keeps a pic of you close."

"What?"

"Well, I guess technically that picture is of you and that gorgeous brother of yours. Looks like you're on some ski trip or something." Naya rolled one shoulder in a casual shrug. The jingle bell earrings that dangled from her lobes let out a soft peal of sound. "You all have on matching red hats. You're in the middle, and they both have their arms around you."

"Breckenridge," Christy managed. "About three years ago. And, ah, I'm sure Wyatt has that photo because it's a good memory for all three of us." They'd laughed like maniacs on that trip, mostly because Forth couldn't ski worth a damn. Neither could she. She and her brother had spent most of the time falling on their asses. Meanwhile,

Wyatt had zipped down the slopes like a pro. He'd been particularly adept at snowboarding.

"All three of you. Sure." Naya pursed her lips. "So you're totally fine if I walk across the room, grab the hot doc, and tug him two steps over so he'll be beneath the mistletoe with me?" Her index finger extended and her cherry-red fingernail pointed across the room.

And Christy's head swiveled back toward Wyatt. She looked first at him, then two steps over. Dammit, there was mistletoe hanging from the ceiling. Who'd put that up? Wasn't that an HR problem in the making?

Naya took a step forward. "Let's go test things."

Christy moved into her path. An automatic side step. The move had Christy turning her back to Wyatt.

Naya laughed. "Thought so."

OhmyGod. I'm territorial when it comes to Wyatt. "It's...complicated."

"Is it?"

Yes. Mostly because Christy had been fighting the attraction she felt for years, and then, bam, last night, Wyatt had blown her mind by saying he wanted her, too.

He wanted her.

She had a stalker on her trail.

And she did *not* want another woman kissing Wyatt...

"I can help you uncomplicate things," Naya told her. "After all, it's the holiday season, and I'm all about doing good deeds. Trying to get off the naughty list, know what I mean?"

Christy shouldn't, she really shouldn't say anything else but... "Go on."

Naya winked at her. "Follow these steps for success. First, you priss over there. You grab the man who can't take his eyes off you, you tug him two steps to the right, and then you kiss him under the mistletoe."

"I—" Christy stopped.

Her new, chatty and helpful friend leaned closer. "Though, I give you ten to one odds that you won't have to do the kissing first. Not with the way he's looking at you. Just get the man under the mistletoe, and he'll do the rest."

Christy pressed her suddenly sweaty palms against the front of her pants. Would he? And what would happen if they actually crossed that line? If she gave into the attraction she'd tried to keep hidden? From him. From herself.

Definitely from her brother...*because I've been lusting after his best friend.*

"You are overthinking things, honey," Naya told her. She put her hands on Christy's shoulders. Spun her around. And gave her a little push. "Go get him. Or someone else will."

Oh, no, they won't. Her spine stiffened as Christy headed across the room. Slowly at first, then with more determination. One step. Another. Then a whole, fast rush.

Her gaze collided with Wyatt's. He'd been talking to the guy next to him. A guy who was just as tall and broad in the shoulders as Wyatt, but with sun-streaked blond hair and not Wyatt's dark mane. The man beside Wyatt wore green scrubs and a killer grin as he watched Christy approach.

As she closed in, Christy thought she heard the other guy mutter, "You have it so bad..."

Her brows shot up. "Excuse me?"

"How can you be so bad..." the man said without missing a beat, "as to not introduce me to your friend, Wyatt? Shame on you. Where are your manners?"

Wyatt grunted.

The blond held out his hand. "Axel Bishop, at your service."

She took his hand. A quick shake.

Only he lingered. A not-so-quick shake.

"For God's sake, Axel, let her go." Wyatt yanked Axel's hand back. "Sorry," he said to Christy. "This jackass has no manners."

"I have a ton of manners. Ask anyone." Axel smiled at her. "You're Forth's sister."

She nodded. Her gaze darted to the mistletoe. Two steps to the right. Did the men realize how close they were?

"Axel is part of SOST with me," Wyatt said.

Should she just grab Wyatt by the shirt and pull him over? Too bold?

"I briefed him on what happened with your stalker, and I also made another call to my buddy Finn. Remember I told you I was contacting him earlier? Finn is on the case. We'll have news soon."

And she stopped thinking about mistletoe. Instead, her horrified stare locked on Axel. Wyatt had told him? A stranger? Telling Finn was one thing. Finn was a PI. She'd been on board with spilling her secrets to him. But Axel was—he was—

"It's okay," Axel said. His features softened as he stared at her. "Your secrets are safe with me."

Her shoulders squared. "I don't know you." She felt anger stirring inside of her. *Who else will Wyatt tell?*

"Wyatt does," Axel assured her. "We're brothers in blood and battle. He was worried and just wanted another pair of eyes looking out for you."

Great. So now two men were at that party, fretting over her safety when they should have been having fun. And she could not get past feeling too exposed. Mostly because she *was* private. Had been, ever since her parents' accident. After she'd gotten out of the hospital, the local media had hounded her. They'd wanted to know all about the woman who'd been trapped in the car with her dead parents for over six hours.

Like she wanted to ever think about that time again. Most of it was, luckily, wiped from her memory. But, sometimes, random images from that horrible time would flash through her mind.

Block them. Stop them. Bury the nightmare.

That was her technique. Forget. Try to pretend that she hadn't been in that horribly twisted wreck of metal as her parents were cold and dead in the front seats.

And this current nightmare that was happening to her? She wanted to keep it buried. To pretend it *wasn't* happening.

Only...it was.

Naya had thought Wyatt couldn't take his gaze off Christy. That was the truth, but not for the reason Naya had believed. It was the truth because Wyatt was just worried. Just in protective mode.

If he really wanted you so badly, why wouldn't he have made a move by now?

Something had held him back. Just as something had held her back.

Fear. If things go wrong, I'll lose my friend. Wyatt wasn't just Forth's friend. He was hers, too. "Wyatt is a good man," she said slowly. "I appreciate all he's doing for me." Christy forced a smile. "I think I'll go grab some of that eggnog. Naya was telling me that it was extra delicious." She whirled away. Marched for the nog.

Naya had been watching her, and at Christy's retreat, Naya's mouth dropped open. Then she mouthed...*What are you doing?*

The answer was obvious. Running away. Playing it safe.

Not wrecking one of the few good things she had in her life.

***

"Killer smile," Axel noted. "Even when it's faked. That dimple is *adorable*. Be still my heart."

Wyatt growled.

"She looked at you, then she looked at the mistletoe, then at you again."

His head whipped to the right. Fuck, there *was* mistletoe up there.

"Way to go, Captain Observant," Axel said with a chuckle. "The woman was two seconds away from sidling under that mistletoe with you, then you blew things straight to hell. I swear, you used to be smooth. Or at least, I think you were. But maybe that was just me. Maybe I was the smooth one and you were the one who wrecked the mood by revealing to a nervous woman that you're spilling her secrets left and right."

"Not left and right," he gritted out. "To you and to Finn. That's *it*. I want her safe."

"Do you want her safe...or do you just want her?"

Both.

"Because the mistletoe is right there. She clearly wanted to go under it and if you're not the man for the job, then I can happily volunteer as—"

Wyatt was already walking away. Striding right to Christy as she stood staring down at the eggnog. Not actually getting a glass because she hated the stuff. He knew, he'd seen her when they tried eggnog shots a few years ago. She'd barely been able to get a drop down. Granted, the eggnog at the hospital party didn't have any alcohol added for kick, but he knew Christy still wasn't going to take a drink.

"We both know you can't stand that stuff," he murmured.

She stiffened. Then swung toward him.

He reached down and took her hand. His fingers curled around hers. More like swallowed hers. Did she remember when she'd stopped being taller than him? She'd been fifteen. He'd been fourteen. That summer, he'd shot past her.

And hadn't stopped growing for a long time.

She was delicate and small. He was big and burly. And he'd always known he would have to be very, very careful with Christy. If he ever got lucky enough to put his hands on her.

"Where are we going?" she asked. "Are we leaving already?"

"Not yet." He took her straight back across the room. Wyatt only stopped when he was dead center beneath the mistletoe. Then he turned and faced her. His fingers went right on holding hers. Deliberately, he looked from her face, to the mistletoe, then back to Christy.

Then she looked at him, the mistletoe, then him again. She swallowed.

"Are you going to do it?" Wyatt kept his voice low, but he had the feeling every person in the room was straining to hear them. Hell, maybe even watching them. He'd never brought a date to a hospital function before. But this was different. Christy was different.

He didn't bother glancing around to see if his suspicion about the others was right or not. He kept looking at what mattered.

Christy wet her lips. "Do what?"

Freaking. Precious. "Kiss me under the mistletoe."

She looked back up at the mistletoe. "It's poison, you know."

"Um."

"Why do people kiss under poison?"

"Because they like to live dangerously?"

She kept looking up. "Isn't that what we'd be doing...if we kiss?" Her voice was even softer than his. "Everything will change."

"Yes." It would. *About fucking time.*

"I'd rather have you as my friend than have you as nothing at all." She turned her head away and pulled her hand from his. "This is a mistake. It's—"

He grabbed her hand and hauled her right back against him. All the way against him this time. "I will be your fucking friend forever. Whether this thing between us works out or it crashes and burns." She needed to understand that. "I would never turn my back on you. You matter." She always had. Always would. "But don't you want to see...aren't you curious to know what it would be like? Because I'm curious. Have been, for a very, very long time."

Her lashes flickered. "What if the kiss is terrible?"

His lips twitched. "Can't imagine anything with you being terrible. Kiss me," he dared her. "Let's find out what a kiss between us will really be like." He tried to sound casual. Like he was teasing her. But, he wasn't casual. This moment mattered to him.

And she was seriously thinking a kiss between them would be terrible? Damn insulting. He'd fantasized about her for years. He'd give her a kiss she'd never forget.

But...

She was hesitating. Maybe he'd pushed too far. *Maybe?* Dammit, he had. They were in a roomful of people she didn't know. Fear had to still quake through her because of what had happened at his house. Yet here he was, pushing her because he was a dick. Plain and simple. Dick.

"Forget it," he told her, voice gruff. His hands let her go even though all he wanted was to hold on. "Friends forever, am I right? The three amigos. Me, you, and Forth—"

She grabbed his shoulders. Shot onto her toes. Her hands wrapped around his shoulders, and she hauled him toward her.

Like he really needed to be hauled. He was more than happy to pounce on her. And pounce, he did. His mouth took hers. Not in a crash. *Can't screw this up. Waited too long.* No, not a crash. Softly, tenderly. With more care than he had ever showed anything or anyone else in his life.

She moaned against his mouth, then her lips parted.

His body tightened. His dick hardened even more. His tongue thrust into the sweetness of her mouth.

His control started to crack.

He tasted her slowly. Savored her. You didn't rush a dream. You didn't crush a dream. You relished it. Lick by lick. Kiss by kiss. One stroke of his tongue after the other. He learned her. He drank up her moans. Enjoyed the quiver of her body in his hands.

And wanted so much more.

Wanted to strip her bare. To run first his hands and then his mouth over every single, delectable inch of her body. He wanted to have her come against his lips. Then around his dick.

He wanted her to scream his name and rake her nails down his back.

His kiss became harder. More demanding. Less suave and a bit more savage.

He wanted her to scream his name when she came.

He wanted her to climax again and again for him.

His control splintered a little bit more. His kiss got rougher. Her nails bit into his shoulders. She rubbed against him and—

"Not here," she whispered against his mouth. Then she blinked. Her eyes were wide. Dazed. She pulled back a little.

Then Wyatt heard the applause.

Her face flushed deep crimson. "Oh, no."

Oh, yes. All of his coworkers were giving them a standing ovation. Fabulous. Wyatt could have sworn that he felt his cheeks burn, too.

A hand clamped around his shoulder. "Been saving that one for a while, huh?" Axel laughed. "Dude, restraint. You're in public."

He didn't want to be in public. He wanted to be somewhere very, very private with Christy. But they couldn't run out right now. Everyone would know he was just taking her to fuck.

His body jerked.

Oh, I want to fuck her. His number one Christmas wish. If he could just unwrap Christy this holiday season, he'd be the happiest man in the world.

This wasn't the time. Or the place.

But his hand rose. His fingers slid over her cheek, and he tucked a stray lock of hair behind

her ear. Then he leaned forward and put his
mouth near the shell of that cute, little ear. "Still
just want to be friends?"

She shook her head.

"Yeah, me neither."

CHAPTER FOUR

"They're predicting snow."

Christy couldn't take her eyes off Wyatt. She swore that she could still feel his mouth against hers. Could still taste him.

"I figure it's as close to a white Christmas as we're going to get," Naya continued. "Growing up in New York, I'd get them all the time. Loved to see that snow fall. Down here? If we get snow once every three years, it's like a miracle hit." A pause. "We're a good week away from Christmas Eve, and the weather forecaster said we'd be lucky if the stuff managed to stick on the ground, but I'm still excited."

Wyatt caught Christy's eye. Easy to do since she'd been staring at him.

"Want to know why I'm so excited? It's because I think I might strip down and walk out naked into the snow," Naya mused. "What do you think about me making a naked snow angel? Do you think my neighbors would mind?"

"No, I'm sure they would love that," Christy responded politely.

Naya burst into laughter.

Christy's head jerked toward her.

"Bad," Naya told her. "You have it *so* bad." Her laughter faded, but the smile clung to her full lips. "Of course, after that hot kiss, I don't blame you. Though why you both decided to act all chill and *hang out* at the party after that body-melting kiss, I don't know."

She...yes, she did have it bad. Because Christy still ached. She quaked. And she'd just had the best kiss of her entire life...

With the guy she'd known forever. "It would be, ah, rude to leave—"

"Your man has done his due diligence and put in his face time at the party. If I were you, I'd be ducking out." Naya leaned conspiratorially close. Her earrings jingled. "Aren't you glad that mistletoe was there?"

Insanely glad.

"I put it up, FYI. You are welcome."

"Thank you," Christy said it once. She meant that "thank you" from the bottom of her grateful heart.

"He's coming this way. And I'm thinking he's about to sweep you out of here..."

Her attention flew back to Wyatt. Sure enough, he was closing in. And there was no missing the hot, predatory need in his eyes. Just seeing that burning intensity had her breath catching. What was up with her?

Just a kiss. It had just been a kiss. A very public kiss that had made her want to get him alone in private immediately. The kiss had sent lust surging through her body. Her nipples had tightened. Her sex had ached. She'd wanted to rip off his clothes.

Her brother's best friend.

And she wanted to *rip* off his clothes.

"Ready to go?" Wyatt asked, voice all courteous and casual.

"Sure." Did she sound casual? Or more like...*Yes, please. Let's go. Now. Let's go someplace so we can be alone and see if a second kiss will hit me the same way.*

It wouldn't, right? That had probably just been some...some adrenaline nervousness. Some pent-up need thing. A second kiss couldn't be as good.

"Drive carefully, Naya," Wyatt advised her new friend. "I heard we might be getting some snow tonight."

"Yes, I did hear about that." Naya bobbed her head. "Christy thinks the snow will make for great naked snow angel fun."

Wyatt's lips parted. He didn't speak. He *did* eat Christy alive with his eyes.

"Thanks for that," Christy murmured to Naya.

Laughing, Naya headed toward the eggnog.

"Naked...snow angel fun?" Wyatt seemed to be choking.

"A misunderstanding."

He extended his hand toward her.

She took it, hesitantly, and, yep, that spark of awareness pulsed through her. It slammed around her nerve endings.

"Making snow angels—while naked—is a great way to freeze your ass off," he said as they made their way to the door. "But I'm game if you are."

And the image of Wyatt—totally naked—in the snow, flooded through her mind.

With his left hand, he jabbed the button for the elevator. Christy glanced around. They'd left the staff break area and were near a nurse's station. A small Christmas tree perched on the counter. Garland had been strung over the nearby patient room doors.

The elevator opened. When she stepped inside, she heard faint Christmas music playing.

Wyatt hit the button for the parking garage. He also let go of her hand.

Why did she hate that? Why did she miss his touch? What was happening to her?

"I never planned for our first kiss to be a public affair."

Her breath rushed out. "You...planned for it?"

"Um. About a thousand times. Figured it would be somewhere private. Just me and you. It would be slow and careful. Then you'd tell me it was the best kiss you've ever had in your entire life."

Oh. *It was.*

He cleared his throat. "Only the kiss was super public. And I wasn't nearly as careful as I should have been."

She'd thought he had been. Gentle. Deep. *Consuming.*

"My control cracked. I wanted you naked."

Her eyes had to be huge.

"And, for the record?"

The elevator had reached the parking garage.

"That was the best kiss of *my* entire life," he told her, voice gruff and rough in the sexiest way. "*You* are the best."

So are you. She opened her mouth to tell him those words.

The elevator dinged. The doors slid open.

Wyatt began to walk out.

Say it. "So are you—*Wyatt!*" Christy's words ended in a scream because she'd just glimpsed the figure rushing toward Wyatt. A figure in black, with a dark hood partially over his head.

It was hard to see him clearly because the lights outside of the elevator were out. They'd been on before. When they left the parking garage earlier, the lights had been shining brightly.

Now it was dark, and she could barely make out the figure. Just that he was big, his hoodie seemed bulky, and— "Knife!" Christy shouted.

Wyatt jerked back and grabbed her. He shoved her behind him.

Why was he doing that? Making himself a target while shielding her? "Wyatt—"

The attacker surged into the elevator. Over Wyatt's shoulder, she saw the guy lunging forward with the knife.

She and Wyatt were trapped in that elevator. The man with the knife would have an easy target.

"Mistake," Wyatt snarled just before he attacked. He caught the man's arm and plowed it to the right—toward the elevator's control panel. Then Wyatt drove his knee into the attacker's groin.

The man's pain-filled howl filled the elevator.

The knife fell from his fingers and clattered to the bottom of the elevator.

"Get it!" Wyatt blasted.

She grabbed for the knife.

And Wyatt pushed their attacker out of the elevator. Wyatt followed him in a quick rush. Wyatt drove his fist into the man's stomach. One punch. Then two.

Christy slammed her hand into the red emergency button on the elevator's control panel. Then she hurried out after Wyatt. Her shaking fingers gripped the knife.

The attacker tried to headbutt Wyatt. Wyatt stepped back, dodging, and the man used that opportunity to break away. He ran into the darkness.

Wyatt reached out and grabbed the back of his hoodie. "The fuck you're getting away." And he slammed the guy into...

What was that? One of the cement columns in the parking garage?

The man crumpled on the pavement.

Wyatt stood over him, hands clenching and unclenching. "You're gonna need some medical treatment, asshole," he snapped. "But first..." He crouched next to the fallen man.

They both just looked like heavy shadows to Christy.

"Who the hell are you?" Wyatt demanded. "And why did you attack us?"

Before the man could answer, the thud of fast approaching footsteps had Christy tensing and surging toward Wyatt as she still gripped the knife in her hand. What if a second attacker was coming?

A bright light hit her dead in the face. "Freeze, lady!" A rough shout.

She hesitated and—

"No!" From Wyatt. And he lunged in front of her...*again*. Second time he'd shielded her. "She's with me, Hayes. With me! Got it?"

The light now hit Wyatt. She couldn't see anything about Hayes. The darkness covered him.

"Why are the lights out?" Hayes asked, voice rasping. "Was doing my rounds. Got worried by the dark—"

"There's an unconscious bastard near the column about five feet away. I think he knocked out the lights and then he came for me and my friend—he attacked us with a knife. Use your radio. Get more guards out here," Wyatt urged him.

Hayes swore. Then he started talking on what she figured had to be his radio.

"Lower the damn light." A rumbling order from Wyatt. "You're blinding me."

The light swung toward the column, the one about five feet away. It fell on the sprawled man.

"Christy, do you recognize him?" Wyatt asked. His voice was flat. Cold.

So unlike Wyatt.

She inched toward the fallen man.

"Nope." Wyatt curled an arm around her waist and brought her back against him. "Look at him from here."

An alarm started blasting.

"Did you push the elevator alarm?" Hayes suddenly asked. "Guy at central command is saying—"

"I did," Christy answered. She strained to see the slumped man. His head was turned away. She needed to get a little closer, but Wyatt's hold was unbreakable. "Thought the elevator alarm would send help our way faster."

"Good idea." Hayes grunted. "Cavalry is coming." Hayes moved closer to the man on the pavement. "Is he breathing?"

"Yes," Wyatt said. The reply came out like a growl.

At that moment, the man on the ground let out a pain-filled moan. His head turned fully toward them.

"Christy, do you know him?" Wyatt asked again. "Is that Jesse?"

She stared blankly at the man's face. Hayes's light fell straight on him. "No," Christy said, completely honest. "That is not Jesse but..." Her head tilted. "I have seen him before." She sucked in a breath. "He's one of the waiters at Jesse's main club, Eclipse." The stark light fell on his features. The hawkish nose with its piercing. The spider tattoo that crept up his neck. Yes, that tattoo—she definitely remembered the tattoo. "I remember him." A jerky nod. "I remember *him*."

***

"He had her picture." Rage twisted inside of Wyatt. Rage had been twisting and growing in him ever since the jerk with the knife had lunged inside of the elevator. "A detective found it on the guy. A worn picture in his wallet." He glared across the parking garage. A now well-lit parking garage. The broken lights near the elevator—because they *had* been smashed to hell and back—had been replaced by maintenance. Hayes had gotten more security guards to respond ASAP, and the cops had come racing to the scene, too.

The perp was gone. Long gone.

"You broke his nose," Axel said.

Wyatt shrugged.

"And three of his fingers."

"Maybe that will teach him not to attack innocent people with knives." His eyes narrowed as he watched Christy finish what had to be her *fourth* interview with the cops. This time, she was talking to the female detective who'd seemed to take charge of the situation. Geraldine Belle. Geraldine had been the one to disclose to Wyatt and Christy that she'd found a photo tucked inside the pocket of the guy's wallet. A picture of Christy.

"I also think I heard he had a broken rib," Axel noted casually, like he was talking about the weather.

"How about that."

"You don't seem concerned."

I'm not. His head turned toward Axel. "He had a knife. If she'd gone out of that elevator first instead of me, he could have slashed her with it. *Her.* So, no, I'm not particularly concerned that the bastard got an ass kicking. What does concern me is the fact that the jerk worked for Jesse Mitchell, the prick ex of hers I told you about before. I'm trying to figure out if this creep tonight is some freaking errand boy carrying out his boss's orders or if *he* is the one who has been tormenting her all along."

"You really think that Jesse guy sent him after her?"

It was an option he couldn't overlook. When it came to her safety, he wasn't going to relax his guard at all. "Could be...or maybe she was wrong about who was stalking her. Maybe it wasn't Jesse. Could be that his employee saw her with the boss, and *he* got hooked on her. The cops are going to investigate, but, meanwhile, I'm damn well keeping Finn on the case." He would not be stopping until he was sure the threats to Christy had been eliminated. Wyatt snapped to attention because Christy and the detective were heading his way.

Shadows lined Christy's eyes. Deep, dark shadows that he hated to see. Her hands twisted in front of her, and her shoulders hunched.

"Well, Dr. Roth," Geraldine said as she closed in, "for a man adept at healing, you certainly did a great deal of damage to my perp." Her loose, dark hair framed her high cheekbones and curving jaw.

"Self-defense," Christy stated at once. "I told you, that guy came at us with a knife. Wyatt jumped in front of me. He protected me."

The same story Wyatt had told, too. The cops had deliberately separated him and Christy for a time. They'd both been grilled. But they weren't the ones who'd made a trap in the dark for their prey.

"He was waiting for her," Wyatt said, voice flat. Waiting to ambush Christy. A fact that still enraged him. "He'd knocked out the lights. When the elevator doors opened, the only illumination would have come from *inside*. He could see us perfectly, but we couldn't see him. He rushed out and attacked."

"And never said a word?" Geraldine inquired.

"Not a word." The tension in Wyatt's body doubled.

"Huh." Geraldine put her hands on her hips. "According to the ID in his wallet, his name's Ramone Horton. Christy said she recognized him, that he worked at a club called Eclipse in Asheville. Once he finishes getting patched up..." A pause as she stared hard at Wyatt.

"Oh, sorry," he muttered. "Was I supposed to let him stab me? Or Christy?"

"Once he's in talking condition," she continued grimly, "I'll take my turn grilling him. Christy told me about the incidents that have been plaguing her. To me, it looks like her stalker made a very big, very dangerous move tonight. But we have him in custody, and I'm hoping the threat is now over." Her lips pursed as she shifted her attention to Christy. "Based on the information you've given me about your situation in Asheville, I *will* be immediately following up with Detective Langston. I think he'll be able to help me with background on Ramone. As soon as I know more, you will, too." She looked back at Wyatt. "I'm assuming you will keep up your guard duty for the rest of the night?"

"I'm taking Christy home," he replied flatly. "And she will be with me every moment." Every single one. Not down the hallway. Up close where he could keep his eyes on her.

Too dangerous. When that bastard had come at her with the knife...

Unable to hold back a moment longer, Wyatt moved to Christy's side. His arm brushed against her. A little of the tension slid from him. A very, very little.

"Christy told me about her tires being slashed at your place last night." Geraldine nodded. "Seeing as how Ramone came at you with a knife—and a knife was most likely used on the tires—I suspect he's guilty of that attack, too. Guy must have followed her all the way down from Asheville. Some creeps just can't let go." An exhale. Sympathy flashed on her face as she told Christy, "Thanks for your cooperation." Her head inclined toward Wyatt. "You, too, Dr. Roth." She turned away.

Once the detective had rejoined the other cops, Wyatt reached out to Christy. His fingers curled around her shoulder as his gaze swept over her body. "You're *sure* that you're okay?"

"You don't need to check me for injuries again," she murmured, voice weary. "I'm fine. You're the one who faced off against him." A little furrow appeared between her brows. "How are you?"

Enraged. On the edge. Holding to his control by a thread. "Fine," he bit out as he reluctantly let go of Christy.

They both knew it was a lie.

"Ahem." Axel cleared his throat. Axel, who'd been uncharacteristically silent as he stood there and watched the byplay. "My friend, I think you are as far from fine as a guy can be. That adrenaline rush has to be riding you both hard."

"Don't know if it's adrenaline," Christy returned as she pushed back a heavy lock of her hair that had fallen forward. "More like leftover terror. I was so afraid that jerk would hurt Wyatt."

"Uh, I think Wyatt did a pretty good job of hurting *him*. Or did you miss the broken nose, the three broken fingers—"

Her eyes widened.

"The broken rib and—"

"*Thank you*, Axel," Wyatt cut in. "Appreciate your summary." He stepped forward and clapped a hand on his buddy's shoulder. He squeezed. A sign to...*stop talking before you make her even more afraid.*

Axel winced. "Just trying to say—Christy, you don't need to be worrying about anyone hurting Wyatt. He does the hurting. Then, of course, he can always stitch up the perp later. If he feels like it." Another wince. "Did that help things?"

"I don't think it did." He released Axel. "But thanks for trying."

"Always got your six, man. Always." Axel looked at Christy. "It could be over now, you know." His words came in a more subdued tone. His comforting-the-patient tone. Wyatt had heard him use that tone hundreds of times. "Maybe this Ramone guy is the one who was causing all the trouble for you. He was caught red-handed tonight. He's going to jail. If he's the one who was after you—him and not his boss—then your life can go back to normal. You'll be safe."

"I'd like to be safe," she said. But a shiver slid over her.

Wyatt didn't like her shiver. He didn't like her fear. He didn't like her worry. "I'm taking her home. On the drive, I'll talk to Finn. Give him an update on everything that's happening." Maybe the stalker was Ramone. If so, they'd know the truth soon. But if Ramone had been sent to attack, courtesy of his boss...*Nope, not dropping my guard. Not letting her out of my sight until I'm sure the danger has passed.* Wyatt caught Christy's hand. Her fingers felt chilled, so he immediately started to warm them with his own. "Come on, sweetheart, let's go." He lightly tugged on her hand.

She didn't move. "You could have been stabbed."

"Nah. Guy missed me by a mile."

Her body stiffened. "You *could* have been stabbed. And I did this. I brought my trouble to you. Right to your doorstep. Literally."

He rolled his shoulders. "Trouble doesn't bother me."

"A knife attack *should* bother you!" she cried out. "It bothers me! I don't want you hurt. I don't want—"

"She's concerned," Axel cut in to say as Christy's voice rose and attracted the attention of a few uniformed cops still sweeping the scene. "It means she cares, which is great for you. But, clearly, you've kept some secrets from your crush, Wyatt, so let me help you out." He smiled at Christy. "I get it. You've known him since he was some snot-nosed punk trailing around with your baby brother..."

Wyatt's jaw dropped in outrage. "Seriously? You just called me a—"

"He grew up. You grew up. Only in your head, you think he's the same sweet boy you knew. A bigger version. Like, a big old, cuddly teddy bear."

Jeez. Axel was again *not* helping.

"Probably think that because that's what he has always *been* to you," Axel continued in a musing voice. "Sweet. Caring. All that annoying shit."

She blinked. "I...don't find it annoying."

"That's just the side of him you see. Only that's not all of him. He's also the guy who just broke an assailant's nose, his fingers, his ribs—"

"*Axel,*" Wyatt snapped because she did not need another recap of the perp's injuries.

Axel waved away his interruption. "That guy—the brutal fighter—he's the one you need right now. The one with special ops training. The one who knows krav maga, judo, jujitsu...he's the one you want at your side when an attacker comes. He's the one *I'd* want at my side if some bozo tried to take me out. Because Wyatt could break your enemy straight apart and barely break a sweat. Want to know who is really, really good at causing pain?" He leaned forward and revealed, "Doctors. Because we know everything there is to know about the human body. Which places break the easiest. Which nerves can cause excruciating pain. We know exactly how to disable someone like that." He snapped his fingers.

Christy gaped.

"Did that help?" Axel asked her.

She didn't respond.

Axel angled his head toward Wyatt. "I was trying to help."

"Got it. Please stop now. You have helped more than enough for the night."

"Have it your way." A sigh. "But if you need me, you call, got it?"

He knew Axel would have his back in an instant. Right then, though, he just wanted to get Christy out of the parking garage and back home.

Safe.

After mumbling their goodbyes to Axel, Christy and Wyatt climbed into his SUV. He maneuvered around the cops and got them out to the street. Wyatt turned on the SUV's wipers because—sure enough—fat flakes of white snow were hitting the windshield. The weatherman had not been wrong. "Axel was trying to reassure you." He had to defend his friend. "His heart was in the right place."

"When did you become so dangerous?"

He turned to the right. *Always.* "I'm not dangerous to you. You never have to worry about that."

"I worry about you. When I ran to you last night, I didn't think things through. The attacks— they'd just been focused on my business. My home. Me. I-I never thought you could be in physical danger."

He braked at a red light. The fat flakes of snow kept falling. Any other time, he would have thought they were absolutely beautiful.

But he was too furious for beauty. Too enraged for calm. *Christy is in danger.* "I don't care."

"What?"

He turned toward her. Found her staring straight at him. "I will gladly stand between you and any threat. I'd do it any day of the week. I don't *care* about the danger. The only thing I care about..." How could she not have seen this? "It's you."

"Wyatt..."

"It's always been you." The snow fell a little harder. "Every woman I've ever met in my life? I compared her to you. I get that wasn't fair. I get that I have an obsession." Yeah. He'd just said the big, fat ugly o-word. "But I am *not* like that freak who has been stalking you."

"I know that."

"I stayed away, but I've dreamed about you. Fantasized about you." His hold on the steering wheel tightened. "And you need to understand that I would never, ever hurt you."

"I do understand that."

Did she? "I would sooner cut off my own hand than ever do anything to hurt you."

She reached out. Touched his right hand as it gripped the steering wheel. "I know that." Soft. Certain.

His breath heaved. "So whatever new things you learn about me..." Like all the shit Axel had revealed. "Never stop knowing that I am different with you. You don't have to be scared of me. Anything bad I can do I...it would be to protect you. Always."

"I don't think there is anything bad about you."

Oh, but there was. She hadn't seen him at his worst. "I've had you in my head for years. No one else measured up. No one had a smile like you. No one had eyes like you. Or your laugh. No one made me feel the way you did. Hell, I was happier just sitting in front of a fireplace drinking hot chocolate with you than I was even when I was fuck—" Nope. Time to stop. Way oversharing. "I will gladly protect you." Better. Way better. "And I am absolutely *not* leaving you on your own until we are *sure* that the threats to you are over. As it is, I'll already be having nightmares for the rest of my life, wondering what would have happened if you'd walked out of that elevator first."

Her hand rose and pressed to his jaw. "You think I won't have nightmares? He could have stabbed *you.*"

Wyatt snorted. "Sweetheart, you are underestimating my skills. I can take care of myself." His head turned, and he pressed a kiss to her palm. "And of you." *Always, of you.* "So don't think of cutting and running." A hard order. "You're not going to Forth's place. You're not ditching town. You're staying with me." Territorial. Whatever. He was what he was.

Wyatt waited for an argument.

None came.

But Christy did clear her throat. "You should know that the light turned to green a little bit ago."

He looked toward the green light. Shit. Wyatt accelerated. They drove in silence. Tense, hard silence, broken only by the swish of his windshield wipers.

Then...

"Wyatt?"

"Yeah?"

"Thank you for saving my life tonight."

"Don't thank me for that."

"Uh, yes, yes, I do need to thank you for that—"

"What the hell do you think my life would be like...if you weren't in it?"

CHAPTER FIVE

He pulled the SUV into the garage and killed the engine. During the drive back to his house, Wyatt had telephoned his buddy Finn. A gruff, clipped conversation about the attack at the hospital. Finn had asked Christy a few questions, and she'd answered as best she could. Her mind was still spinning from the attack.

That knife came way too close to Wyatt.

And...could it have been Ramone all along? She remembered meeting him a few times. Somehow, he'd always been her waiter when she went in Eclipse, appearing as if by magic.

Was Ramone the stalker or had he just been following orders from his boss?

Wyatt jumped from the vehicle. He started to come around to her side, but she hurriedly exited. That was Wyatt. Always the gentleman. Holding doors. Waiting for her.

Beating my attacker to a pulp.

Her breath shuddered out. Had he really broken the guy's nose? Three fingers? And a rib?

The fight had been so fast, but she could still remember the brutal sound of those punches...

Wyatt unlocked the door leading from the garage to the house. She started to enter and...

"Let me go first," he said gruffly. "After what happened in that elevator, we are pausing the ladies' first routine for a while. I need to make sure no unwelcome visitors are waiting inside."

She peeked into the darkness of his house.

Wyatt hurried inside. The lights flipped on.

She followed after him. Paused to lock the door. To creep forward.

After a fast search... "Clear," Wyatt told her. They both ditched their coats, and Wyatt set the alarm. He walked with her to the den. The soft lights of the tree gleamed. No ornaments. They hadn't gotten around to putting on the ornaments. But to her, the tree looked beautiful just as it was.

She stared at those soft lights. Got lost in them for a moment. Everything was supposed to be happy during the holiday season, wasn't it? Maybe the danger was over. Maybe she could be happy again. Safe. Now that Ramone was in custody, maybe life could be normal once more.

Wyatt's fingers brushed over her arm. "You have to be exhausted."

No, she wasn't. In fact, Christy felt completely wired. Perhaps the adrenaline rush Axel had mentioned was finally kicking in for her.

"Want to shower? Change? Listen..." Gruff. "I know this will seem crazy, but I don't want you sleeping alone tonight."

Her head turned toward him. She was far too conscious of the fast beating of her heart. *Not sleeping alone?*

"It's not safe," Wyatt added and raked a hand through his already tousled hair.

"It's not safe...in your house?" she asked carefully. Just to be sure she understood things.

"I want to be able to keep my eyes on you. I meant what I told the detective at the parking garage. Every moment, I want to be close."

Every moment, hmm? "You just told me to shower. To change. You going to be with me while I do that, too?"

He swallowed. Had she imagined the flare of heat in his eyes? "You think I'm being overprotective." His jaw hardened. "A man came at you with a knife. You already told me that you were stalked in Asheville. You get here and your tires are slashed. You're hunted at the hospital, so—hell yes, I'm overprotective. If I could, I think I'd cuff you to my side. I want to know you're safe. Every moment. And I..." His eyes closed. "I'm not rational when it comes to your safety."

Christy thought about how she'd felt when she feared the knife would slash him. "Fair."

His eyes flew open. "Excuse me?"

"I don't think I'm rational when it comes to your safety, either." She didn't back away from him. Christy stepped closer. Her body brushed against his. "You have kept secrets from me."

"I—"

"You've been in war zones. You've been in the heart of danger, yet whenever I asked about you and your team, you skimmed over things with me in the past. Told me it was just a bunch of training missions." Her jaw tightened. "You lied to me."

Wyatt winced. "Christy…"

"Do you know how scared I would have been, how worried, if you'd told me the truth?"

He leaned toward her. His forehead pressed lightly to hers. "Why do you think I didn't tell you?"

She had to blink quickly because tears filled her eyes. "How long have you been protecting me?"

"It's kind of what I like to do."

"Don't keep secrets." A whisper. "Not from me. I want to know about you."

"Because I'm…your brother's best friend?" His head lifted. His electric gaze locked on hers.

She shook her head. No.

"Because…I'm your friend? Practically family since I've known you for so long."

Another shake of her head. "You're not family."

Pain flashed on his face.

Oh, dammit, the *wrong* thing to say. He'd lost his parents not long after she'd lost hers. A heart attack for his father, and then cancer for his mother. Christy knew how much their deaths had hurt him. How he'd been gutted as he watched his mother struggle every day. She'd stood with him at both of their funerals. Held his hand. And hurt for him.

Wyatt had no siblings. When she'd lost her parents, she'd grieved with her brother. Forth had always been there for her. But Wyatt…he didn't have a brother or a sister. Not even any cousins. He'd been alone.

Forth is his family. His best friend. And he has me. Wyatt will always have me. "I'm not explaining things right." She reached out and gripped his hand. "I mean I don't feel..." This was so hard. She was messing it up. "You aren't Forth."

"No. I'm not." Flat.

"And you're...yes, you are a friend. One of the best friends I've ever had."

He waited. Watched her.

"But I thought we agreed we were done with being just friends." She wet her lower lip. Then looked upward in frustration. "Where is some dang mistletoe when you need it?" Definitely not hanging from his ceiling. She supposed she'd just have to do things the hard way.

"Christy..."

Her stare flew back to catch his. "Wyatt, just kiss me."

And he did. But it wasn't like before. Before, it had been a kiss meant to tempt. To seduce. One that had made her toes curl and her body tighten with yearning. He'd savored and sampled and seduced, and she'd basically gotten lost in him. The best kiss ever? Oh, yes. Or at least, she'd thought it had been.

Only this kiss...

Their second kiss...

It blew the first away. Because there was no control. No restraint. Just raw, primitive passion. He kissed her with demand and passion. So much lust. Fierce. Consuming. Her nails dug into his shoulders, and she rose onto her toes as she tried to get even closer to him and kiss him back with the same wild demand.

There was no audience. There was no applause.

Except in my mind. Because in my mind...this man just got a standing ovation.

His tongue took. Tasted. She moaned. Her body rubbed against his, and there was no way she could miss the hard dick thrusting toward her. He was turned on. She was practically melting. And all he was doing was kissing her in front of a partially decorated Christmas tree.

"I want you naked," he rasped against her mouth. A sexy, dark, demanding rasp. "I want to kiss every single inch of you." A hungry shudder worked the length of his body even as his hands closed around her waist.

Then he picked her up and—

Moved her back?

She gaped.

But, yes, he'd just moved her back. A good foot. He put her down, and she felt the tree branches brushing against her back. Then he squared his shoulders and stared at her.

Silence.

His eyes seemed to eat her alive. But he'd just put that weird foot of space between them.

She had to swallow the lump in her throat. "Distance makes it hard."

Those incredible eyes of his narrowed.

"How are you going to kiss every inch of me with all this space between us?" A fair question, she thought.

His hand flew up, as if he'd reach out to her, but he stopped. "You ready to cross that line?" Gruff. "Because there will be no going back for me. I told you the truth before. You're a fantasy that I've had for a very long time."

They needed to get things moving along. Desire was about to shake her apart. She caught the hem of her blouse and lifted it over her head. Christy tossed her top onto the floor. "Wyatt, Wyatt, Wyatt...what makes you think you're the only one with fantasies?"

A muscle flexed along his suddenly locked jaw.

She kicked out of her boots and ditched her socks. Was he truly not going to help her along? Did she have to do all the heavy lifting here?

No, he confessed earlier. He told you everything. He's wanted you for years.

Show him that you want him, too.

Her hands went to the front of her black pants. She unhooked the button. Slowly lowered the zipper. His eyes followed the movement of that zipper. His hands clenched and unclenched.

She let the pants fall, then casually stepped out of them. Casually? Right. Her heart raced so hard she expected it to burst from her chest at any moment. "You were right. Red is my f-favorite color," she said, stuttering a little because she could only pretend to be confident for so long.

Her bra was red. Her boyshort panties matched.

And Wyatt hadn't moved.

So, how long was she supposed to stand there, backlit by the tree? She'd kinda hoped that once she started stripping, he'd take the hint and—

"Beautiful," he rumbled. "Every single inch of you. Best Christmas present ever."

"Wyatt, I—"

He surged forward. Kissed her again. Deep and hard. Put his hands on her and without her blouse between them, she could feel the powerful warmth of his touch right against her skin. Heat swept through her. It tangled with the need and adrenaline and everything else spilling through her blood. She didn't want to think about tomorrow. Didn't want to think beyond this moment with him.

I won't lose him. He'll always be my friend. He had to be.

This is more. We both said we'd take more.

His fingers slid up her body. Moved to her back and unhooked her bra. Then he caught the straps. Pulled them down. Tossed away her bra.

Her nipples were already tight, hard peaks. From the slight chill in the room? From the arousal spreading through her? From—

His fingers teased her nipples. Her breath choked out as she leaned into his touch.

"Fantasies don't compare to reality." He kissed her neck. Stroked her breasts. "Let's go upstairs—"

"No." Her head shook. "Right here." Beneath the lights.

"Baby, I won't fuck you for the first time on the floor."

Her eyes widened.

"But I will touch you. And I'll get you to come for me right here beside the Christmas tree."

And he was touching her. His fingers slid down her body. Eased beneath her panties and dipped down, down...until he was rubbing her clit. Pushing a finger into her. She shot onto her toes, and her hands clamped around his arms as she tried to balance herself. "Wyatt!" Okay, maybe going up to the bed was a better idea because she wasn't sure how much longer her trembling legs were going to hold her.

It was just...heat of the moment and all. When she'd said "right here" to him, it had been because she didn't want to stop and think or hesitate or worry about why what they were doing might be a mistake.

A mistake can't feel this good.

Nothing had felt this good. No, this right. Things felt *right* with Wyatt.

"Easy. I've got you." Then he—he lowered before her. Went to his knees. His hand pulled from her.

She hadn't meant that the man needed to *stop*. "Uh, Wyatt..."

He leaned forward and kissed her through her panties.

She shivered. And it wasn't from the faint chill in the air she'd felt before. Chill. What chill? All she felt now was hot.

"These have to go. As cute as they are. But you know what, how about I just move them to the side a bit?" And he did. He scooted her panties to the side, and his mouth was on her. He'd angled her hips with one hand, opened her up to him, and his tongue slipped over her clit and dipped into her.

If he hadn't been holding her, she would have fallen. No doubt about it. Her knees had turned to mush, and she would have slammed onto the floor.

But he had her. A fierce grip as he tasted her, and her breath came faster and faster.

"Not good enough," he growled. "Need *everything*."

Then her world spun as he lifted her up, took her to his oversized couch, and he yanked her panties off completely. They hit the floor somewhere. She didn't even look to see where. She couldn't. He'd spread her out and partially climbed between her legs and he was feasting. Licking with his tongue. Strumming her clit over and over again with his fingers at the same time. There was no holding back. No stopping the release that pounded through her body. One moment, she was on the precipice, a tightrope getting ready to snap, and then she was falling. Gasping and choking out his name as her hips bucked against his mouth, but he just kept right on devouring her.

She didn't tremble. She quaked. Her whole body jerked, and she grabbed the nearby couch cushions so hard that Christy wondered how she didn't rip them apart.

She might have also screamed. Hard to know for sure.

But his head slowly lifted. And when she saw his face...

Wow. No one had ever looked at her quite that way. Primitive lust. A claiming stare. This was not the sweet boy she'd grown up with.

This was a man she didn't fully know.

A man who'd just given her the best orgasm of her life. Hands down. As in, not even close.

"Now, I'm fucking you."

Fuck away. She almost said those very words. That was how far gone she was with blissed-out orgasm pleasure. But she didn't get a chance to actually make that statement because he'd risen and plucked her from the couch and into his arms. He carried her easily, just as he had the previous night when he'd taken her up the stairs. And if the man wanted to carry her, who was she to argue? Especially since Christy wasn't sure her legs would work that well.

She looped her arm around his neck. Held on. And then, because his neck was right *there,* she leaned forward and gave him a little kiss. Then a lick. A nibble.

"*Christy.*" He stopped. Halfway up the stairs. "I'm trying not to fuck you right here."

Oh. On the stairs? "Think you could?" Her words were almost a dare.

His head turned. "I could fuck you anywhere."

Promises, promises. But something about that blazing stare told her he meant every word. Before she could say anything else, Wyatt was double-timing it up those remaining stairs. Holding her tightly, and she didn't play again, even though she really wanted to kiss him again. To lick and stroke but—

His control is gone. She knew it. She'd seen the truth on his face.

He kicked open the door to his bedroom. Darkness waited inside. He took her straight to the bed. She thought he'd drop her. He didn't. He lowered her carefully. Slowly. Her back hit the soft comforter, and she realized that while she was completely naked, Wyatt was still fully dressed.

"You need to lose the clothes," she told him.

But instead of stripping, he...he left her.

The bathroom light flipped on. Squinting, she pushed up on her elbows and saw him reaching for—oh, right. Condoms. He grabbed a few. As in, a handful, and he came back to her. He left the light on in the bathroom so she could see the dark outline of his body as he closed in. He tossed all but one of the condoms onto the nightstand.

"Think we'll need them all?" Christy asked, then bit her lip.

"They'll be a start."

He wasn't serious. Men just said boastful stuff like that. Being all confident and cocky, and sure, it had been a *while* for her, longer than she actually wanted to admit, but he didn't mean they would actually use all those condoms in that one night. It looked like at least five condoms waited on the nightstand.

The hiss of his zipper had her gaze flying away from the pile of condoms and back to him just in time to see—

Oh, wow.

Big. Thick.

No underwear. Just his dick. A fully aroused, ready dick. He ripped open the small packet he'd kept.

Not so fast. Christy surged toward him. Her fingers wrapped around his cock, and she pumped him. Base to tip. Once. Twice. He was hot. *Strong.* Her head lowered, and she wrapped her lips around the head of his cock. She licked. Sucked.

"*Done.*" He pulled her back. Tumbled her onto the bed. Shoved her thighs apart. Then he rolled on the condom and positioned the head of his cock straight at her core.

She reached for him.

He caught her hands. Threaded his fingers with hers. Pushed them back against the bed as he lowered over her and drove himself into her. All the way in with one long, hard thrust.

She cried out because it had been a while and he was built along very sturdy, big lines.

Wyatt immediately stiffened. "Christy?"

"Give me..." A quick pant. "Just a sec."

"I'm hurting you. Fuck this." He started to withdraw.

She locked her legs around him. "No, fuck me." Another pant. "Just...give me a second, would you?" Talking was no small feat. "Been a while."

"Define."

"What?"

Through clenched teeth, he gritted out, "Define 'a while.'"

"A year." She should be honest. "More like two."

"Fuck."

"Yes, I would like to do that," she assured him. "I'm trying to adjust. You're just...bigger than I've had before, okay?"

A choked groan escaped him.

He let go of her right hand. He lifted up a little, as much as he could lift his body considering she'd wrapped her legs tightly around his hips, and his fingers eased down between them. He went for her clit. Strummed her. Rubbed. Caressed her over and over until her body relaxed and softened once more beneath his.

"Better?" Wyatt demanded.

"It would be better if you withdrew...and thrust again. And again..."

He withdrew. Not all the way out. The head of his cock stayed in her, and then he drove deeply inside again. Not as hard as before.

He withdrew.

Drove into her.

Controlled thrusts.

She wanted *uncontrolled*.

Her free hand flew up and curled around the back of his neck. Christy pulled him toward her. "I'm okay. Give me everything."

"I don't want to hurt you—"

"Everything." She kissed him. First his mouth. A hot, open-mouthed kiss. Then his chin. His neck. She licked. Sucked.

He broke and gave her everything.

Frantic drives of his hips against her. His cock slammed into her again and again. There was no pain. There couldn't be. She was too slick now. Too eager. He'd worked her clit—was *still* working her clit with his wicked fingers—and she came almost immediately. A powerful explosion as her release surged through her and definitely had her screaming out his name.

He didn't stop. Just kept plunging into her. Faster. Harder. The bed rocked. They rocked. Over and over. All she could do was hold on for the wildest ride of her life.

He stiffened. Jerked. Wyatt pumped into her and bellowed her name.

Her heart pounded so hard. The drumming filled her ears. Her legs remained wrapped around his hips in the aftermath. She didn't want to move. Didn't want to stop. Nothing had ever been this good. Nothing had ever consumed her this way.

His head lifted. She wanted more light so she could clearly see his face. His eyes.

"Can you take me again?"

He was still in her so—

He withdrew. Christy couldn't help the murmur of protest that broke from her.

"*Can* you take me again?"

"Yes," she whispered.

He stalked to the bathroom. Ditched the condom. And came back to her.

Her gaze darted to the pile of condoms he'd left beside the bed. "We're not...we're not really going to use all of those?"

His fingers reached out and trailed over her thigh. His touch sent a quiver through her.

"I've been fantasizing a long time," he told her. "One or two fucks isn't going to come close to satisfying me."

How many condoms were left on the nightstand?

"Spread your legs for me, baby."

She'd closed them automatically when he went to the bathroom. And now, she slowly parted them.

He reached for another condom.

***

The blast of hard rock music woke him.

Wyatt jerked and nearly shot upright in bed. Only to realize that something—or rather, a sexy someone—lay sprawled half over him.

The rock blasted again. A familiar song from the 80s. Because Forth Sharpe was a big fan of the old, big-hair bands of the 80s, and he'd programmed that ring tone into Wyatt's phone.

Christy's brother is calling. And she was sleeping through the call like the dead.

Wyatt's left hand flew out and grabbed the phone from the nightstand. He swiped his finger over the screen to stop the blaring of the music and put the phone to his ear. "Hello?" A whisper.

"What in the hell is happening?" Not a whisper. More of a shriek. "Where is my sister? She'd better be close."

Oh, she was close. Super, super close.

"Close as in you had better have your *eyes on her!* I got the message about what's been going on!" Forth was barely stopping for breath. "This is bullshit! Bullshit!"

Bullshit. Check.

"She's been stalked, and she didn't tell us? We are her family! Her only family!"

She snuggled a little closer to Wyatt and kept right on sleeping. Hell. He'd probably worn her out last night. *Sorry, sweetheart. I was too hungry for you.*

"I'm her freaking brother! And, hell, you might as well be—"

"I am not her damn brother!" Wyatt snapped back. Snapped, snarled. Same thing. But that had also been a very *loud* snarl, and Christy gave a jerk.

He waited for her lashes to open. They didn't.

Okay, mental note. She sleeps very, very soundly.

"What?" Forth demanded. "You're gonna say you don't care about Christy—"

"Oh, I care about her all right." Care. Hah. Like that was the correct word. "But I'm not her brother. No blood relation. I do *not* think of her as my sister."

"But she's family!"

She was his world.

And she was naked in his bed. "So, uh, Forth, we need to talk..." He leaned forward. Damn but she smelled delicious. Strawberries. Sweet, sweet strawberries.

"Absolutely, we do. I'm flying home. I'll be there in about, hell, twelve hours? I've got to land in Atlanta, but then I'll drive back home. You watch my sister until then. You do that for me?"

"She's not getting out of my sight," Wyatt replied. Forth could be assured on that point. "She's...ah...she's sleeping right now. It was a big night." *I fucked her too hard*. Oh, shit. Axel had been right. Forth was going to try kicking his ass. "Uh, buddy..."

"Dammit, man, you are such a good freaking friend to me," Forth exclaimed. "What the hell would I do without you?"

A good freaking friend. Who'd just fucked Forth's sister. "There is really something you need to know."

"You have my sister?"

"Oh, I have her." And he never intended to let her go.

"Your eyes are on her?"

"Every inch. On her."

"Then when she wakes up, you tell her I'm on my way. Tell her I trust you completely."

Wyatt winced. *Maybe you shouldn't trust me so completely*.

"Now, what do I need to know?" Forth demanded. "What were you trying to tell me?"

Wyatt's right hand lightly stroked Christy's bare shoulder.

"Wyatt? What do I need to know?"

Wyatt's forced his jaw to unclench. "I'd kill anyone who tried to hurt her."

"Damn straight. I would, too. *Thank you*, man. Thank you."

"You don't need to thank me."

"Yeah, I do. You're my best friend in the world. Have always been. And you're going above and beyond for my sister. Above and beyond. I will find a way to repay you for this, I swear it. You name what you want. Just name it, and it will be *yours*."

"Well, there is one thing—"

"Got to go. *Protect her.*"

Forth hung up.

Wyatt gripped the phone. His gaze remained on the one thing that he wanted.

Christy's eyes slowly fluttered open. Her head turned a little, and she smiled at him.

Just name it, and it will be yours.

Interesting. What would Forth say when Wyatt told him that he wanted Christy?

CHAPTER SIX

"Snow," Christy blurted.

An absolutely adorable furrow appeared between Wyatt's dark eyebrows. "Say again?"

"I forgot about the snow." She'd just woken—in his bed, cuddled up to him—and her entire world felt off-kilter. So she'd said the first thing that came to her mind.

Okay, fine. That was a lie. The first thing that had come to her mind was...*We used all the condoms on the nightstand*. Insane. Amazing. But it had seemed safer to go with... "Snow. It was snowing when we came in last night." She sidled away from him and took the sheet with her because Christy was, in fact, buck naked.

His blue eyes watched her as she crawled from the bed and wrapped the sheet around her body. A faint smile played at his gorgeous lips, and his eyes twinkled as he tucked his hands behind his head. "You thinking about running out and making that naked snow angel you and Naya were talking about?"

Her mouth opened. Closed. "Ah, no. That was a joke." Maybe it had been? She didn't quite know Naya well enough to be sure about that part. "I was just thinking about...seeing if the snow stuck. Maybe making a snowman with you." *Maybe doing something that would ease me from what feels like an extremely awkward morning after*.

"It's Mountain Brook, not Asheville. Highly doubtful that anything stuck."

She'd already rushed to the window and peered outside. Her breath slid out.

"You wouldn't, by any chance, be trying to avoid talking with me about what happened last night?" Wyatt asked, his voice all calm and cool. Completely casual.

One hundred percent, I am. Because she had no idea what to say. Should she roll with something like...*Thank you for the best orgasms of my life. All eight of them?* Had it been eight? She'd lost count. They'd had sex over and over and everything was a blur and... "You have really good stamina." Oh, no. No, no, no. Wrong thing to say.

A sharp bark of laughter burst from Wyatt. "Thanks. I try."

Her cheeks burned.

"But I have to say, that whole stamina bit had a lot to do with you. When you've wanted someone as long as I've wanted you, once just isn't enough."

She spun toward him.

He hadn't changed position. Wyatt still lounged in the bed, with his hands folded behind his head. Looking as casual as his voice had sounded. He flashed her a grin. "Hi, there."

"The...snow stuck." Like a lot of it had. Sure, it might melt in a few hours, but it had stuck for the time being.

"Your brother just called."

Her hand clutched the sheet tighter to her chest. "*What?*"

"You slept right through the phone call. You're beautiful when you sleep, by the way. Beautiful when you're awake, too."

She sucked in a quick breath. "Forth...called?"

"He's on his way home. He'll be back tonight. Wanted me to tell you that."

Forth is coming home. Her drumming heartbeat seemed to echo in her ears.

"Also said for me to tell you that he trusts me completely." Not so casual. Rougher.

Her bare feet inched closer to the bed. "You didn't tell him about us?" No, surely Wyatt hadn't told Forth what they'd done. You didn't just bluntly announce something like that over the phone.

You didn't just bluntly announce it *any* way to Forth. She already knew...*he will freak out.*

Wyatt sat up. The comforter fell to his waist. His muscles flexed and rippled, and one man should really not be that hot. Surrounded by the dark bedding, all of his golden skin just seemed extra lickable. His blue eyes appeared brighter than normal, and with that morning shadow lining his hard jaw...

No. Stay focused. Stop thinking about how gorgeous he looks.

"Tell him about us? What part of *us* are you referring to? The *us* as in...you're staying with me so I can protect you? Or the *us* as in...we fucked all night long?" He climbed from the bed.

Automatically, her gaze fell. Right to his cock.

"Oh, sorry. Guess I'm still naked." Utter unconcern.

Still naked. Still aroused. How—after last night, how? "Shouldn't you be, ah, finished?"

He blinked and then burst into laughter. Loud, long laughter.

Christy's foot tapped. She hadn't been making a joke. He still wanted her? It hadn't been a sort of one-night-get-it-out-of-your-system thing for him?

That laughter slowly tapered off, and then he closed in. Still naked, he closed in like a lion stalking prey. His hands lifted and curled around her shoulders. "One night with you isn't going to finish me. Not in any way, shape, or form. I want more. One hell of a lot more."

"But...Forth is coming home."

Those brilliant blue eyes narrowed. "So?"

"So..." So she didn't know what to say.

His nostrils flared. "For the record, no, I didn't tell Forth that I had the insane pleasure of fucking you all night long."

Insane pleasure? Yes, it had been rather insane. She'd never felt such pleasure. She'd screamed. She'd raked her nails down his back. She'd begged for more.

He'd given her more. A lot more.

"But he will have to know *all* about us, sooner or later."

Later, please. Much, much later. Dealing with a stalker was one thing. One horrifying thing.

Dealing with her brother when he found out what she'd done with his best friend? Yes, saving that for later seemed like a good plan.

"What do you want here, Christy? For me to pretend like last night didn't happen?"

Her head jerked. "No." She'd never be able to forget their night together.

"You want us to go back to being just friends?" Flat. "Because I should tell you, I don't really see that happening."

For some reason, those words made pain knife through her chest. "I thought you said you'd always be my friend. No matter what happened." Now he was saying he wouldn't?

His hold tightened. "Christy..."

The doorbell pealed.

Literally, saved by the bell. Saved before she said something she couldn't take back. Even though she had no idea what to say. Or what to do. Or how to feel. The hours with him last night had been like a beautiful dream. Every touch and sensation intensified. But in the bright light of day...

What happens next?

The doorbell rang again. That was what happened next. "We need to get that," she whispered.

"We aren't finished."

No, they'd have to figure things out. Would they tell the truth to Forth? Keep it secret?

"No," he said with a hard shake of his head. "I'm not your dirty little secret. You sure as hell aren't mine."

"Wyatt—"

He let her go and turned away even as the doorbell pealed yet again. Whoever was at the door was damn persistent. Wyatt snagged his phone from the nightstand and swiped his finger over the screen. Inching closer and peering over his shoulder, she realized he was staring down at one of those doorbell apps. He had a perfect view of his front door, and the person who kept insistently ringing the bell.

"Geraldine," Christy said as she recognized the other woman. "Detective Belle. Something has happened with my case." Her stomach twisted with a surge of alarm and hope.

Wyatt was already grabbing a pair of sweatpants and tugging on a t-shirt.

Christy rushed to get dressed, too. Only—her clothes were in the other room. So she yanked on his oversized robe.

They flew down the stairs. Wyatt got to the door first. After flipping the locks, he yanked it open.

Geraldine's hand froze in the act of ringing the bell again. "Took you long enough," she grumbled as a puff of misty air drifted from her mouth like smoke. "I'm out here, freezing my ass off on your porch, and meanwhile you are...oh." Her eyes widened. She'd just gotten a look at Christy. And the oversized robe that kept trying to slide off her shoulders. "You were otherwise occupied. I see."

Too late, Christy tried to smooth down what had to be seriously wild hair. And the fact that her robe was falling off because it was too big? Yes, wonderful. The picture she and Wyatt made had to be exceedingly clear. *Lovers*.

"I was on my way home after one very long night, and I thought I'd stop by and deliver the news personally," Geraldine informed them. Her knowing gaze slid between Christy and Wyatt. "Guess we all had a long night, hmm?"

"Come in, Detective," Wyatt said because they were still in the entrance area and the icy air blasted inside. "Warm up."

"No, my news is short and sweet." She squared her shoulders. The scarf she wore slid a bit to the left. "You're safe now, Ms. Sharpe. Ramone confessed to everything. He's your stalker. He's the one who destroyed your studio in Asheville. Who broke into your house. He's even the one who slashed the tires on your Jeep when you arrived here in town." She pointed back toward the Jeep.

The tires weren't slashed any longer. Wyatt had gotten new tires for her.

"Ramone confessed to it all. The bad guy is locked away, and you can go back to Asheville and know that you'll be safe."

Back to Asheville? Automatically, her gaze swung to Wyatt.

He stared straight at the detective. "Thank you for letting us know," Wyatt replied. "Appreciate it."

"He gave a full recounting." Geraldine pulled her fluffy, tan coat closer. "Provided details that only the perp would know. I spoke with Detective Langston in Asheville to verify everything. Ramone is our guy." A shiver slid over her. "Now,

I'm going home to defrost and crash. You two have a good holiday."

"Thank you!" Christy hurried to exclaim as Geraldine turned away. "I'm very grateful for all of your help!"

Geraldine glanced over shoulder. "I'm glad you're safe and that Ramone is in a cell. Stalker cases don't always end this way." Sadness flickered over her face. "Wish they did." A long exhale that sent another puff of cold, smokey air from her mouth.

Christy crept closer to Wyatt. Why did just being near him make her feel safer?

The detective tossed her hand up in a wave and then carefully made her way over the snow to her dark sedan. The engine growled.

Christy watched the detective leave. Shivers skated down her spine, but those chills weren't necessarily from the cold. *Stalker cases don't always end this way.* Yes, Christy knew she was lucky. Lucky and grateful. Both to the detective and to Wyatt. "Thank you," she whispered.

He caught her hand and tugged her deeper into the house. "I get that you love the snow—it was the first thing you thought of when you woke up this morning—but how about you at least put on shoes before you go out there?" The door shut. He flipped the locks.

Another shiver chased over her. "It wasn't the first thing I thought of."

Wyatt frowned at her.

"You were the first thing." She needed to stop being afraid and nervous and just tell him the truth. "I thought about how much I enjoyed being with you. How the night felt like a dream, but it wasn't. One of the worst nights of my life turned into the best, because of you." Well, great. Now she was just confessing all. But why not? Her shoulders squared. "You saved me."

"I didn't."

"You did." And she'd never forget those terrifying moments. "You put yourself between me and a knife. How am I ever going to be able to repay—"

"You don't." A growl. A very adamant one. "You don't repay me. Because you don't owe me anything. Don't you get it? It's *you*. You, Christy. You need me, I'm there. You're scared, you're worried, or, God forbid, you're hurt? *I am there. Always.*" His chin lifted. "I meant what I said last night. Making love to you didn't change it. I will always be there for you." He walked toward the den. Toward the Christmas tree that waited in the corner.

Helpless, she followed him.

With his back to her, Wyatt paused in front of the tree. "How about if you ever have a problem again, you come straight to me? You don't let me find out after you've been terrorized for months. You tell me right away."

She tugged on the belt of his robe in a vain attempt to tighten the oversized fit.

"Because you can tell me anything." He still wasn't looking at her. "I'd keep every secret you had. Hell, when I said I wasn't going to *be* your dirty secret? Total lie. You want to fuck me in secret? Want to keep the truth about us quiet? I'll do it." He swung toward her. "That's how much I want you. I want you *more than anything* in this world. I'll take you any way I can get you."

"That's...not what I want."

"No?" He yanked a hand through his hair. "Then what do you want? What is it—exactly—that you want? Because I am dying to know."

She fiddled with the belt again. *You.* Only she couldn't blurt that out.

"Why don't you think about it?" he rumbled. "And when you know, then you come to me."

He's not afraid. He's not holding back. So why was she? Why had she always held back with him? And when was she ever going to stop?

Maybe...maybe right now.

She untied the belt.

His lashes fluttered. "Christy?"

"I want you. That is the one thing that is crystal clear in my mind." Her stomach was twisting and churning and her fingers shook. Part of her was so overjoyed she could hardly stand it— *the nightmare is over. I don't have to be scared any longer! My stalker is in jail.*

But another part...another part was scared but for an entirely different reason. Scared because she was about to take a big step. With Wyatt. The biggest step of all.

She was going to risk her heart with him.

Her shoulders rolled. The robe began to dip.

Wyatt bounded toward her. He caught the robe before it could fall. His fingers trapped the soft cotton fabric against her shoulders. "I should tell you, I have fantasies similar to this. You come to me, wearing a coat and nothing underneath it.

When you arrived at my doorstep, at first, I thought you just *were* a dream."

"I'm not."

"You are to me."

She licked her lips. "I don't have anything on underneath this robe."

"Christy..."

"The detective said the danger is over. You don't have to protect me any longer. I could walk out the door and go back to Asheville right now."

His hold tightened.

"But I don't want to go anywhere," she told him. "I want to spend Christmas with you."

His stare searched hers. "What about your brother?"

Giving the news to Forth wouldn't be pretty. He'd rage. And what she feared most was that she'd hurt him. She didn't want Forth hurt. Didn't want Wyatt facing his anger. *But I want a chance with Wyatt*. After swallowing, she tried to inject some humor and tease, "I saw you fight in the parking garage. Pretty sure you can handle him." An effort to lighten what felt like an ever-so-tense mood.

But Wyatt grimly shook his head. "Not gonna fight Forth. But...hell, I might have to let him get in at least one good punch. I'll take a hit any day for you."

She rose onto her toes. Her lips feathered over his jaw. "I don't want anyone hurting you."

His hands rose.

The robe fell.

And a phone rang.

Christy's body jerked.

The phone rang again. Upstairs. Wyatt's phone. The ringing seemed to echo through the house. She remembered that he'd dropped the phone right before they'd rushed down to meet the detective.

"Could be the hospital," he rasped. "I have to get it. I'm sorry, baby." His lips feathered over her temple. "Be right back."

"Wyatt..."

"Don't even think of putting that robe back on. *I will be right back.*"

***

If the damn doorbell wasn't ringing, then his phone was. Fuck it. He'd been having a *moment*. An actual, real moment with Christy, and she'd been about to play out one of his penultimate fantasies.

He shoved open the door to his bedroom and grabbed the phone. He wasn't technically on call, but if there was an emergency at the hospital—

Wait. That's Finn's number. Wyatt whipped the phone up to his ear. "Bro, one day, I am going to have to tell you just how bad your timing was—"

"He's gone."

"What?"

"Jesse Mitchell? He's not in Asheville. Disappeared sometime during the night. No freaking clue where he is."

Wyatt rubbed the knots in the back of his neck. "You were watching him?" Wyatt had known that Finn was heading to Asheville, but he hadn't realized Finn was setting up some kind of stakeout situation with Jesse.

"I had an associate keeping eyes on Jesse until I could arrive. If the prick was trying to hurt the girl you've been mooning over for years, I wasn't gonna take chances." Frustration rumbled in Finn's voice. "My guy isn't an amateur. No one should have gotten past him, but Jesse did. He's in the wind, and you need to be on alert."

Oh, he already was. Every muscle in Wyatt's body had tightened at the news. "The detective I told you about last night? Geraldine Belle? She just left my place. Came by to tell us that Ramone Horton made a full confession. According to her, he's the one who's been stalking Christy. Geraldine is considering the case closed."

Silence.

"Finn?" Wyatt prompted.

"You want me off the case? You really think this is all over?"

Wyatt hesitated. "Ramone was the one with the knife. He was the one with her picture. The one waiting in a dark garage. Everything points to him." Except...*This is Christy.* "But no, I don't want you off the case yet." When it came to Christy, he wouldn't take any chances. "Dig a little more. Dig and see if you can figure out just where Jesse went." Because the fact that the jerk had vanished in the middle of the night?

Big freaking red flag.

"On it," Finn replied. "You just stay on her."

Wyatt hung up the phone. "Not a problem."

The wooden floor outside of his door creaked. Wyatt spun around. Christy slipped forward as she entered his bedroom.

"Wyatt?" Concern flashed on her face. "Was that the hospital? Is everything all right? Do you have to leave?"

She'd just started to relax. Just had actual relief on her face moments before as she'd confessed that she wanted to spend Christmas with him.

With Geraldine's visit, Christy had hope. The shadows had finally left her eyes. They could be happy.

But not if I scare her. Not if I give her a new reason to look over her shoulder.

And maybe Jesse wasn't the one after her. Maybe Ramone is our guy. "Everything's fine," he told her. He closed the distance between them. "And I'm not going anywhere."

Her smile flashed.

He reached for the robe. Tugged it open. *Hello, fantasy turned reality.* "Except to bed, with you."

CHAPTER SEVEN

Christy ran out of the back door. Her booted feet thudded down the back porch steps. Dark clouds swirled overhead, and she glanced back quickly. There wasn't going to be much time.

She bent down low, and her gloved hands flew out around her. *Hurry, hurry, hurry*...

"Christy?" Wyatt's sharp voice. "Baby, where are you?" His feet thudded down the stairs. "*Christy?*"

In a flash, she rose—and launched her hastily rolled snowball right at him. He'd been turned to the left, but at the last moment, he looked her way. His blue eyes widened in surprise. Then...

Nailed.

The snowball burst apart as it hit him right in the chest.

Laughter bubbled from her. She just couldn't help it. "Payback," Christy cheerfully called to him. Oh, yes, she was feeling cheerful. Super cheerful. Amazing sex would do that to a woman. And more snow had fallen. Like a Christmas miracle for them. "Do you remember how many times you would nail me with snowballs when we were kids?" She scooped up another hunk of snow and began rolling it in her hands. "You and Forth would gang up on me. I remember one time when we were on vacation together in Viriginia, and I walked out of the cabin—you guys hit me with like ten balls all at once."

His hands rose, and he slowly wiped away the snow from his chest. "Been wanting revenge for a long time, have you?" Low. Rumbly.

She paused in the act of rolling. Because there was something about his expression... "Wyatt?" A bit of nervousness slithered through her.

"How about a final battle? Me and you? Winner takes all?" He bent and began rolling his own snowball with his hands. A much, much bigger ball.

"No need." *I am not getting hit with that ball.* "I think we're even now." *Not even close.*

He kept rolling that ball. And the look in his eyes...

Uh, oh.

They'd had sex. Phenomenal sex. Toe-curling, body-humming sex. He'd made her breakfast. They'd laughed and talked and...while he'd been getting dressed, she'd snuck out for a little, well, fine, okay, she'd call it exactly what it was— revenge.

Wyatt stalked toward her. The massive snowball remained cradled in his hands.

"You're not going to throw that at me," she said.

One eyebrow quirked. "I'm not?"

"No." She'd slid one hand behind her back. The hand that hid the ball *she'd* rolled.

"And why not?" He was right in front of her now.

Soft snowflakes began to fall. They teased her cheeks. Her nose. Her lips. Her head tilted back as she peered up at the sky. Everything around her seemed to sharpen and crystallize. This moment seemed...special. Different. Suddenly far more important than a silly snowball fight.

Her ball fell from her fingers. "Because we don't want to fight." She looked back at him. "Not when we could be doing something far more fun." She reached out and took the ball from him. Or, tried to take it. The ball crushed between their fingers. "Ever made love in the snow?"

"Christy."

"You have a privacy fence. Not like any neighbors can see us." Ever since the detective had left, joy had been growing inside of her. Joy. Hope. Freedom. Everything seemed possible now. The danger was gone. Wyatt wanted her. They were spending Christmas together. She hadn't been this happy since...

Before my parents died. Before everything fell apart. Before I woke up and was surrounded by death. No, no, she wasn't going back there. She'd never go back to that dark place again.

"No one can see," Wyatt agreed in a voice that was barely more than a growl. "But, sweetheart, you will freeze your delectable ass off out here."

The snow fell harder. He was probably right. They'd both freeze their asses off. Not a good plan. Not a—

His mouth crashed onto hers. His tongue pushed past her lips and the last thing she felt was the cold. Christy grabbed tightly to him. She rose onto her toes and kissed him back with desperate passion. This was what she wanted. Him. Right then. Right there. Snow was falling, and she'd never kissed someone beneath a snowfall. Just as she'd never kissed anyone beneath mistletoe, not until Wyatt.

But she was kissing him now and tasting both Wyatt and the snow. She pressed her body to his as tightly as she could. All she wanted was to feel him. Every single inch of him. She'd fuck him there or inside. Beneath the Christmas tree. On the bed. She'd—

He lifted her up against him. Christy wrapped her legs around his hips, wrapped her arms around his neck, and she held on tightly. The snow fell as he carried her back into the house. At least, that was where she thought they were going.

Christy lifted her head to see. *Yep, back to the house.*

Then she started kissing his neck. Licking. Nipping. Loving the way he'd groan for her.

He kicked the back door shut, then immediately turned and pinned her against the door. His hands grabbed at her coat. Wrenched it open. And then he was shoving her shirt up. Shoving her bra out of his way.

This...this intensity felt different. More frenzied. More desperate. His fingers were cold— *icy*—as he touched her, and a quick gasp tore from her lips.

"Warned you," he panted. "If we'd stayed out there, your ass would be frozen. Now, your ass is just mine."

"Promises, promises," she threw back.

He stilled. His head lifted. His gaze locked on hers.

And...something *was* very much different. She could see it. His eyes had never blazed quite that way before.

"Yes," he told her, "that is a promise. You're mine." He spun her away from the door. Put her on the table. Then proceeded to strip her. Right there. Her boots. Her socks. Her coat. Her gloves. Fast, recklessly, as if he had to get her naked.

Like he hasn't had me that way already...

But...

The urgency in his touch felt so different to her.

And he wasn't stripping. He remained completely dressed in his sweatshirt and jeans and boots, but he had her totally naked on the dining room table. Seriously, the dining room table, and he grabbed her thighs and spread them apart. "*Mine,*" Wyatt said again.

Then he put his mouth on her.

Part of her was still chilled from the snow. But when he began to lick and kiss and thrust his tongue into her core, the cold vanished. Her body burned with heat and passionate need, and she practically melted on that table for him.

His fingers plucked her clit, then worked her over and over while he kept licking. Feverishly, he tasted her. Seemed bent on consuming her. And Christy couldn't hold back the orgasm that plowed through her. It was too strong. Too consuming. She opened her mouth and screamed when she came.

Her body sagged against the table.

And she forced her eyes to crack open.

Wyatt loomed over her. His hands gripped the edges of the table. His eyes were on her parted thighs.

"Fucking beautiful."

She wet her lips. "Aren't you...coming in?" *In me. Now. Here.*

His gaze lifted.

Her breath seemed to freeze. So many emotions swirled in his eyes. So much need. No, beyond need. There was more in his stare. So much—

He unbuttoned his jeans. Hauled down the zipper.

His dick surged toward her.

He reached into his pocket. Knowing Wyatt, he had a condom stashed there. Though, at the rate they were going, they'd definitely need to restock soon.

But... "No."

His head whipped up.

"I barely have gotten a taste. Fair is fair, Wyatt. And I want *everything*." She climbed off the table. Not very gracefully, but, whatever. She climbed off, then she went to her knees before him.

"*Christy*..." His hands clamped around her shoulders.

Her hands reached for him. Her fingers curled around the long length of his cock. Her mouth eased toward him, and she lightly blew over the straining head.

His hold tightened on her.

She opened her mouth and took him inside. Last night, she'd tasted him, but just briefly. He'd pulled away before she could fully savor him.

Now, this was her time.

Her tongue licked over him. She moaned at his tangy taste and took more of him. Maybe she was awkward, but he didn't seem to mind. In fact, Wyatt seemed to love every stroke and lick. Her gaze darted up to his face, and she saw the savage lines of need that had been carved into his expression.

He tried to pull her to her feet.

She didn't stop.

She kept licking. Sucking. Taking.

"Baby, I can't hold back."

She didn't want him to hold back. That was the whole point. She'd gone wild against his mouth, and now it was his turn. He could—

He hauled her to her feet. Lifted her up. Put her on the table. He had a condom out and on in seconds, and he plunged deep into her.

They both moaned.

Then it was nothing but a feverish rush. Bodies hitting. A desperate drive to release. She was slick and sensitive, and every stroke of his cock into her had Christy quaking. Her inner muscles clamped greedily around him. Her heels dug into his ass. She arched against him. Her climax built and built and—

Pleasure.

It exploded through her.

Through him.

She saw the pleasure fly across his face. Felt the hard jerk of his hips as he came inside of her. Her hands flew up and her fingers pressed to his cheeks. He kissed her. Deep. Hard.

The same way he'd fucked her.

The same way—

His mouth tore from hers. "I love you," he said.

And her heart seemed to stop.

CHAPTER EIGHT

He'd fucked up.

Majorly.

Wyatt figured he could blame the verbal slip on the mind-blowing sex. Because, seriously, how was a guy supposed to think clearly when he was barreling his way straight to heaven with the woman he'd wanted forever in his arms?

So the love bit had slipped out. Not the plan. The plan had definitely *not* been to come on too strong. But then again, the fact that he kept pouncing on her and driving his eager cock into her every chance he got? *Too strong.*

When it came to playing things cool, he just sucked. At least where Christy was concerned. *I waited too long. Waited and she was in danger, and I will not do that shit again.* There would be no more holding back. Not when it came to her.

With her, he would be all in, all the time.

"I can't believe you didn't tell me!" Forth's voice rose even as he hugged Christy for what had to be about the tenth time.

Because, yep, they were at Forth's place. Night had fallen. Her brother had come barreling home moments before, and he'd swallowed Christy in a bear hug at first sight. Right in the driveway. They'd eventually made it inside the house, but then Forth had hugged her again. And again.

Wyatt watched them from his perch near the now crackling fire. Unlike Wyatt's house, Forth's place had been fully decked out for the holidays. But Wyatt doubted Forth had actually hung the garland or wreaths or put up all of those carefully matching ornaments. Nah. His money was on Forth hiring a professional decorator. Forth had never been the overly hands-on type.

"You should have told me!" Forth blasted as he squeezed the breath from Christy. "I would have come to Asheville immediately. I would have brought you here! I would have done *something*."

Wyatt cleared his throat. "She needs air, buddy."

Forth's head whipped toward him. "What?"

"You're squeezing her too tightly." Christy would never complain to her brother, so he'd do the deed for her. "Give her air."

Forth's grip eased.

Christy shot Wyatt a grateful look. She also pulled in a deep gulp of air.

He tipped his head toward her. *Baby, I'm always watching out for you.* Did she get that? He wasn't just doing some protective duty during the holiday season. He wanted always. With her.

"Why didn't you tell *us*?" Forth demanded. "Wyatt and I are your family."

Wyatt stiffened.

Nodding briskly, Forth added, "You're just as much of a sister to him as you are to me—"

Christy's grateful look transformed into one of horror.

"Nope," Wyatt called out clearly. "Not my sister. Don't think of her as a sister. Never have. Never will."

Forth let go of Christy and whirled toward him. "What is your deal?" He took an aggressive step toward Wyatt. "You know you love her!"

Wyatt forced his back teeth to unclench. His eyes were on Forth now, but he could feel Christy's stare. *You already told her. Not like you can pull those words back now.* "Sure I do," he said easily. Absolute truth. He loved her, body and soul. "But she's not my sister, and I don't love her that way."

"Fine!" Forth's hands flew into the air. "You love her like a friend—"

No, I just love her. Done. No use fighting it.

"Is that better?" Forth huffed. "We don't need semantics right now. We need answers. We need to know why Christy didn't trust either of us enough to tell us what was going on." His shoulders suddenly slumped. "If you don't trust us to protect you, who do you trust?"

Now Wyatt surged away from the fireplace. "She does trust me." No way would she have given herself to him so completely if she hadn't. And there was not an inch of her body that he didn't now think of as *his*.

"It wasn't about trust." Christy's voice came out soft when Forth's had been angry and hard. "I just didn't want to bring my trouble your way. I thought I could handle things."

"But you never have to handle things on your own! That's what family is for." Forth raked a hand over his face. "I hated being out of the country when you needed me." He exhaled on a long sigh. "Wyatt, I am forever in your debt. Know that. Like I told you on the phone, *anything* you want, you just say the word. It is yours."

Wyatt met Christy's stare. A faint flush covered her cheeks. "Well..."

The doorbell rang.

Seriously? "Why the fuck is a doorbell or phone always ringing lately?" Sure, if it was Christy ringing his bell in the middle of the night—*down for it.* But now people were just annoying him with all the bells going off left and right. He had a big confession to make. He, Christy, and Forth needed to clear the air, STAT. Like ripping off a band-aid. He needed to tell Forth...

I'm fucking your sister. I'll give you one punch, but that's it. Just one. And then I will—

The bell rang again.

"Who the hell is that?" Forth muttered as he took a step forward, obviously intending to go see who was ringing his doorbell.

Wyatt waved him back. "I'll get rid of them." Whoever it was. He marched for the door. "You need a doorbell camera," Wyatt threw back over his shoulder. "How do you not have one of those? Seriously? You're the tech-crazy guy from MIT, and you don't have a doorbell camera?"

He didn't catch Forth's response because he'd just swung open the door.

A stranger stood on the doorstep.

Tall, with dark brown hair and a hard jaw. He wore a black leather coat and battered jeans. The porch light fell onto his face, and when he saw Wyatt, he stiffened. His gaze swept over Wyatt, and he said, "You must be the brother."

Wyatt blinked. "Excuse me?"

The man's shoulders straightened. He cleared his throat. "I'm Jesse Mitchell. I'm a...friend of your sister's."

The fuck you are.

"I need to see Christy."

Wyatt moved to fully block the doorway. "That shit is not happening. You need to get the hell out of here, now." His hands fisted at his sides.

"Look, I understand that she's probably told you about what's going on, and as her brother, you're protective—"

"I am *not* her brother."

"Wyatt?" Forth called from behind him. His footsteps rushed forward. "Who is it?"

Jesse Mitchell frowned. "Not her brother? But I'm at the right house?" He took a step back and glanced at the number on the siding. "Three-oh-eight. That's right. The address for Forth Sharpe. I've been told that Christy is here, and I want to see her—"

"Not fucking happening," Wyatt informed him flatly. Rage burned in each word. "You're staying away from her."

"Look, I get the protective vibe." Jesse winced. "If I had a sister, I would be—"

"She's not my sister. She's my fucking girlfriend. *Mine.* Got it?" He took a lunging step out of the house. "She's been through hell, and from where I'm standing, it seems like you followed her—stalked her—down here. So you need to get back in your car and you need to leave. Now," he snarled. "I will not be telling you again."

There was a quick gasp from behind Wyatt. He looked back and saw Forth, with his jaw pretty much on the floor.

My fucking girlfriend.

Well, at least that part was done. "Save the punch," he muttered to Forth. "Got other things to handle first."

Christy hurried toward the door and Wyatt. Her brother threw up his arm, stopping her before she could get to Wyatt. Her eyes were wide and worried and—

"Christy!" Jesse called. He'd caught sight of her. "I'm sorry! I swear, I had no idea what Ramone was doing. If I'd known he was after you...*I'm sorry!*"

The guy had been warned to leave. Instead of leaving—

Jesse lunged for Christy. During that lunge, he slammed into Wyatt.

Such a bad move.

Wyatt grabbed the guy mid-lunge. He caught Jesse's arm and twisted it behind the bastard's back.

Jesse cried out in pain.

"Not breaking anything," Wyatt assured him. "Not yet. You hit me first, so I'm defending myself and throwing your ass *off* the porch." With his hold on Jesse, Wyatt shoved the jerk forward.

Jesse slipped on the ice. Ice now, not snow. The snow had melted earlier, but when temps had dropped with the sunset, the moisture had turned to slippery ice. Jesse slipped and fell on his ass. Scrambling to get up, he shouted to Christy, "He's my brother!"

What?

"Ramone—he's my brother! He's had problems in the past. I knew about them. Tried to stop him. Tried to help him." His head hung forward. "I thought he was better, I swear it!"

Wyatt glared at Jesse. "How did you know Christy was here?"

Jesse's head lifted. "I have to bail him out."

That wasn't an answer to Wyatt's question. But maybe Ramone had called him. The guy would have gotten a phone call, after all. *But how did you know Christy was at Forth's tonight?*

"Who the fuck is he?" Forth demanded as he edged closer. He'd left the house and made his way out onto the porch. "What's going on?"

"That's Jesse Mitchell," Christy's husky voice drifted from the house as she crept onto the porch with Forth. "He's the guy I...I thought he was my stalker."

Jesse looked toward the porch. Toward Christy. "It wasn't me. It was Ramone, and I promise you, he will not hurt you again. I will make sure he gets more treatment. The best care. He won't hurt you or anyone else again." He took a step forward. As if he'd go up the steps. Go to Christy.

Hilarious. *Not happening*. Wyatt moved into his path. "You're not getting near her."

Jesse blinked at him. He was far enough away from the porch lighting that half of his body now remained in shadows. "You're..."

"The boyfriend," Wyatt finished for him bluntly. "The guy who stood between her and your *brother* when Ramone came at her with a knife. I'm the man who loves her. And I'm the man telling you that as long as I'm breathing, you are not getting near her." Rage. Jealousy. A bitter mix. Most of all, though...*I don't trust this guy*. "How did you know she was here?"

"Christy mentioned her brother to me once. I know how much she loves him. It wasn't hard to find his address when I got to the area. And I *had* to come when I found out that Ramone had been arrested." His gaze darted up to the porch once more. "No matter what, family matters, doesn't it?"

One of the slats of wood on the porch groaned as Christy walked forward a bit more. "You never told me that Ramone was your brother," Christy said.

"Half brother." Jesse exhaled and rolled his right arm. The one Wyatt had twisted. "It's complicated. I don't tell just anyone about our relationship."

"Because he has a history of stalking and terrorizing women?" Wyatt pounced. "You trying to hide your ties to him?"

"I'll get him help. I came here tonight to say how sorry I am." Jesse's chin lifted. "He won't bother you again, Christy. I give you my word."

"Great. You gave it." Wyatt did not like the way Jesse kept looking at Christy. *Way too much longing.* "Time for you to go."

Jesse glared at him.

Well, at least you're not looking at Christy any longer. Glare at me all you like, asshole. You hate me? Trust me. The feeling is mutual.

"You need to go," Christy advised Jesse.

Wyatt sent him a savage smile. "You heard the lady. Want an escort?" Because he would be happy to shove the man across the ice again.

But Jesse backed up. "I'm going, I just..." Again, he focused on Christy. Need flashed on his face. "I wish things had been different. I never intended for anything like this to happen. I-I really admired your work. I admired you."

Stop looking at her like you want to eat her alive. "You have five seconds to get in the car," Wyatt ordered him. "Five. Or you will be getting that escort—"

Jesse whirled away. He stomped back to the black Range Rover that waited. He nearly fell on his ass twice, but soon he was in the vehicle. The headlights flashed brightly before he reversed down the drive.

Wyatt didn't move, not until that vehicle was long gone. The cold didn't matter to him. Rage burned from the inside. "I don't trust that bastard."

"That...that was the guy you dated back in Asheville." Forth's words were halting. "The club owner that you thought might be the stalker. And he was just at my front door."

Wyatt spun at Forth's words.

He found Forth and Christy standing on the edge of the wrap-around porch.

"His brother is the one who came at you with a knife?" Forth added. He let out a low whistle. "And now Jesse is showing up here, telling you how sorry he is..."

Christy's hand curved around the white post near the steps.

"No wonder you lied to him." Forth squared his shoulders and inclined his head toward Wyatt. "Good job, buddy. Let the bastard believe you and Christy are an item. I don't want him anywhere near my sister. He can think she's involved with someone new, and he can stay the hell away from her." He reached for Christy. "Come on, sis, let's get inside. My fingers are going freaking numb out here from this cold."

Christy didn't move. She stared at Wyatt. "Wyatt isn't the type to lie."

Forth's head wrenched toward Wyatt.

Here it comes.

Wyatt braced his legs apart. He unfisted his hands. After all, Forth did deserve one free hit. "I wasn't lying."

Forth bounded down the steps.

"I've wanted your sister for a long time—"

"You are my best friend—"

"I'm serious about her. This isn't some fling—"

"She's my sister—"

"And I would live and fucking die for her, I—"

Forth's fist came flying.

"No!" Christy screamed. Wyatt hadn't even realized that she'd flown off the porch because he'd been so focused on Wyatt, but she suddenly shoved between them. "Forth, you are not hitting Wyatt!"

No, he wasn't. Forth's fist was already flying, and it was heading straight for *her*.

Oh, hell, no.

Wyatt grabbed Christy and tucked her hard against his body, just as Forth's fist plowed into his side.

CHAPTER NINE

Christy felt Wyatt shudder against her. He didn't groan. Didn't let out any sound of pain at all, even though she'd just heard the distinct thud as Forth hit him. Wyatt had wrapped his body around her. Shielded her.

"No one hurts you," he whispered.

"What the fuck?" Forth's shocked tone. "Christy? I almost hit—jeez, Christy!"

Wyatt slowly let her go. His gaze swept over her. "You good?"

"No. No, I am not good." Her breath heaved out. She pointed a shaking finger at her brother. "My asshole brother just punched you! A gut punch. You—the man who *saved* my life! Forth, are you crazy?"

Wyatt turned to look back at her brother.

Christy took that opportunity to rush toward Forth—and to jab him in the chest with her pointing index finger. "You don't hit him! Not ever again, understand me?"

"You're...you're not sleeping with him," Forth announced, like saying the words would make them true. "Christy, you are not sleeping with my best friend."

Her eyes narrowed. "I'm a grown woman. Your *older* sister. I don't think I quiz you about your sex life." *So don't tell me what to do with mine.*

"He's my best friend!"

"And he's the man I want!" she yelled back. Whoops. An actual yell.

Her brother shook his head.

"We should take this inside," Wyatt murmured. He'd just been punched, but there wasn't even a hint of pain in his voice. "Go inside before the neighbors start coming out to catch the rest of the show."

Her head swiveled toward the nearby houses. Were the neighbors already watching? Probably. More like very, very likely.

"You're not coming in my house," Forth snapped. "You're...you're fucking my sister?" A dazed question. But then, angrier, he thundered, "You're my best friend and you're fucking my sister!" Now *he* was definitely yelling.

Christy stopped poking him. She wrapped her hands around his shoulders and shoved him back toward the house. "Inside. We will talk about this like adults *inside* the house."

"No, no, he's not coming inside." Rage flowed in every word. "I trusted you!" Forth fired angrily at Wyatt. "I asked you to protect her. Not to have sex with her! This is *Christy!* She's my world. You know that. You know—"

"What *you* need to know," Wyatt cut in, and he wasn't angry. Wasn't raging. He was just speaking. Flat. Cold. "What you need to know is that she's my world, too."

Christy let go of her brother and spun to face Wyatt.

"You are," he told her simply. "You have been for a long time. Why do you think I basically lost my mind when I found out you were in danger? Nothing bad can happen to you. Nothing bad because you have been the *good* thing in my life for longer than you realize." Then he backed up a step. "Only the last thing I want to do is cause trouble between you and your brother. You two...you go talk. I'll give you some time alone. You need that."

"Wyatt..." She didn't want him leaving.

"You talk, then I'll have my chance to explain things. I'll give your brother a bit to cool down. We both know he gets angry as hell, then cools down five minutes later."

"I'm not cooling down!" Forth bellowed.

Oh, the neighbors could not have missed that.

"You're not getting any other free punches." Again, flat and cold. No rage at all in Wyatt's voice. "I gave you one. That's it. I'm not dicking around with her. Christy knows how I feel."

Christy knows how I feel. Did he...did he really...Suddenly she could hear his earlier words running through her mind. So, so clearly...*I love you.* She'd worried those had been heat-of-the-moment words. That he hadn't really meant them.

But, he had...?

She took a hesitant step toward Wyatt.

"You know how I feel," he told her. His hand lifted and cupped her cheek.

"Get your hand off my sister!"

"Go screw yourself, buddy," Wyatt returned without missing a beat. "In five minutes, you'll regret everything you're saying. I know you. And you know me." His stare flickered to Forth. "You think I'd risk our friendship over some casual fuck? There is *nothing* casual about the way I feel for her."

There was nothing casual about the way she felt for him, either. "Wyatt, I don't want you leaving."

"You need time with him. And he and I need to cool down a bit before someone says something that can't be taken back." His fingers slid gently over her skin. "I don't want to lose his friendship, but I'm *not* losing you. You're it for me."

Her hand rose and curled around his wrist. "Wyatt..."

He pulled away. "Need to check on one or two things." Gruff. "Go inside, baby. You'll catch a cold out here." He turned away. Headed for his SUV.

"Good thing I know a really awesome doctor," she called after him.

He stilled.

"You're coming right back? Promise?"

"Let him go," Forth muttered behind her. "You and I need to talk, *now*."

Yes, they did.

Wyatt glanced back at her. "I'll be back before you can miss me." He sent her a smile. But it seemed forced. Tight. So unlike Wyatt.

Forth tugged on her shoulder.

She didn't move. Not until Wyatt was gone. And when his taillights disappeared down the road, she felt the oddest pang in the pit of her stomach.

"I can't believe you had sex with him! Christy, what the hell? Why would you—"

"Stop being a dumbass." Clipped. She was shivering and shaking—both from the cold and her own anger—as she turned on her heel and marched back into the house.

Forth dodged her steps. He almost nearly slipped on the ice but caught himself at the last moment. As soon as he crossed the threshold of the house, he slammed the door shut. "I want an explanation! Now! Like, how long has this been going on?"

She turned away from the brightly decorated den and focused on him. "Since yesterday."

His jaw dropped.

But now was the time to be completely honest. "Only I'm thinking I've actually been in love with him for a whole lot longer than that."

His mouth opened, but no sound came out.

"Sometimes you just don't realize what you have, what is right in front of you..." She rolled her shoulders in a shrug. "I realize it now. So you're going to need to deal with the situation."

"You...you think you're in love with him?" Forth seemed to be choking.

Her eyes narrowed. "Why am I telling this to you?" Wyatt had told her how he felt, but she'd been so stunned. And afraid that—*did he mean it?*

Is it true? "Wyatt is the one I should be telling." Wyatt was the one she *would* be telling.

"Y-you're gonna tell Wyatt that you love him?" Each word was gasped out.

"Yes." Determined. "And if you have a problem with it, too bad. Because no other man in my life has ever measured up, no other man has ever felt right, and I think I know why." She'd just been too blind to see it. "No other man was...Wyatt." As soon as he got back, she would tell him. A wide smile spread across her mouth. "No other man will ever be him," she said. "Wyatt is it for me."

***

"Yeah, Finn, I'm telling you, the bastard is *here.* As in, he just showed up on Forth Sharpe's doorstep," Wyatt spoke into his Bluetooth as he drove down the dark road. "I'm on my way to the police station to figure out what the hell is happening." The main reason he'd agreed to leave Christy? It wasn't about giving Forth time to cool down—screw that shit. He could handle Forth's anger any day of the week. He'd left to figure out what in the hell was happening with Ramone. He'd left to make sure there were no more threats to Christy. "Jesse said the guy was getting out on bail! If he's getting out, I want to know it. There is no way that sonofabitch is getting close to Christy again."

"Jesse Mitchell is already in Birmingham?" Finn demanded. "That's where he went when he vanished?"

"Uh, yes." He'd just told the guy that bit of intel. "And did your research turn up that he is Ramone's half brother?"

"No. That shit is news to me."

Bright lights flashed in Wyatt's rearview mirror. His eyes automatically narrowed. Yes, okay, the road was extra dark. There were patches of black ice. You didn't need to go flashing someone. "And Jesse said he knew about Ramone's problem. That he'd tried to get his brother help before. Jesse came for Christy, saying he was apologizing, but something felt *off*."

"He went straight for Christy?"

"Straight to her brother's house. And the way he looked at her—" But Wyatt broke off. The bright lights had flared even more. Because the joker behind him was lunging closer. Speeding? On an icy road? What the hell? "Got to call you back, man. Roads are bad, and I've got some jackass on my tail."

"Why did things feel off to you?"

"What?"

"You just said something felt off with Jesse. What was it?"

It was the way he looked at her. "Maybe I'm just a jealous bastard but..."

An engine snarled.

His eyes flew to the rearview mirror. To the too bright lights. The car wasn't just close. "Fuck!" Wyatt cried out.

It wasn't just close. It was—

Ramming him.

The other driver slammed into the back of Wyatt's SUV. The tires slid but didn't catch traction as the vehicle spun. It had hit a patch of ice on the road, and it slid and spun and slid and—

The driver slammed into him again.

Tires squealed. Metal crunched.

Christy!

Her image flashed in his mind.

freedom is the vehicle again. If had felt a pinch of
...on the road...ugh, stiff and sore and slid under
the dirty steering wheel into...gn.
They squeaked into...hen, then had
christy.
forming a tear...t...

CHAPTER TEN

"I'll have to apologize to him," Forth mumbled.

Christy lifted a brow. "Oh, definitely. A profound apology. Maybe even one that involves you being on your knees. You *hit* him."

Her brother grimaced. "It's just...it's you. He's my best friend and...it's *you.*"

"You've never punched any other guy I've dated."

"He's my best friend," he said. His lips pulled down. "I can't believe I punched my best friend."

"He'll forgive you." She peeked out of the window for the sixth time. It had been way more than five minutes. "He'll come back, and he'll forgive you." *And I can tell Wyatt that I love him.* No, she wouldn't do it in front of her brother. She'd do it when they were alone. She wanted the moment to be special.

"You're...really serious about him?"

Christy glanced back at her brother.

"As in, forever serious?" His head tilted as he waited for her answer. "Because...he's a good guy, Christy. Don't play with him if you don't mean it."

"Oh, so now you're protecting *him*?"

His lips thinned.

"Forever serious," she replied. "Yes, I want forever with—"

Her phone was ringing. Frowning, she hurried for her bag and pulled it out. Christy didn't recognize the number on the screen, and she started to ignore the call because it was probably just a random telemarketer but...

But some instinct had her finger sliding over the screen. She put the phone to her ear. "Hello?"

"Christy? Is this Christy Sharpe?"

A telemarketer. She should have ignored the call. Trying to be polite, she responded, "Uh, yes, but I'm not interested in—"

"I think something happened to Wyatt."

Her heart seemed to stop. And she realized that she'd heard that voice before. The deep, masculine tone was familiar.

"This is Finn," he said even as she made the connection. "I was talking to Wyatt on the phone. He was on his way to the police station to figure out what was happening with Ramone, and I heard a crash."

Her body swayed as she felt all of the blood leaving her face.

Her brother's eyes were on her. He bounded forward and threw out a hand to steady her. "Christy?" Concern flashed on Forth's face.

"I don't know where he is," Finn said. "Can you get out there and trace the path he might be taking? He'd said he was just with you and left to go to the station. Go find him. I'll pull strings and see if we can track his phone but...but it went dead."

Dead.

Crash.

"No." A soft plea.

"You...you can't trace his path?"

Oh, hell, yes, she was tracing his path. She'd meant...*No, nothing is wrong with Wyatt. Nothing can happen to Wyatt. Please, no.* She choked down the lump in her throat. "Wyatt isn't dead. We're going to find him, now."

"What's happening?" Forth whispered. But he'd clearly caught her fear.

She lowered the phone a little. "Wyatt...Wyatt has been in an accident."

All of the color left Forth's face.

***

"Trapped, aren't you?"

Wyatt's eyes fluttered open. Something sharp shoved into his chest, and his legs—dammit, they were pinned. He reached out and punched against a deflated airbag.

"You went off the road. With some help. From me."

His head turned. That voice was coming from close by. Wyatt tried to take quick stock of the situation. His SUV had rolled over and over. He remembered that. Remembered metal crunching. An airbag slamming into his face. The passenger side window had been broken out. So had one of the rear windows. The SUV seemed smashed to hell and back.

I remember the other driver hitting me. Not just once. Several times after Wyatt's SUV had started spinning on the ice. And that voice...

I know it.

"Christy's boyfriend," Jesse Mitchell said, his disgust plain. "I always suspected there was someone else. She just—she wouldn't let go with me. Froze me out each time I tried to make a move. I just didn't realize her boyfriend was quite so close to home for her."

That sonofabitch tried to kill me. Wyatt didn't speak. He was too busy planning. First, he had to get his legs free. And then...

There's something stuck in my chest. Not near my heart, thank Christ. Several inches over. But it's deep in me, and when it gets pulled out, the blood will start flowing. He couldn't really assess his injuries. He felt freaking numb.

But one thing was clear...

I have to stop this bastard.

"When we were at Forth's place, you told me that as long as you were breathing, I wouldn't be getting near Christy." Smug laughter. "I can assure you, you won't be breathing much longer. And I *will* be getting very, very close to Christy."

The hell he would. *You will not touch her.*

"You're gonna die out here. No one will find the wreckage for days. Then when they do, everyone will think it's such a shame that you lost control of your car on an icy road and died." Jesse's shadowy form moved closer. And then he slammed something into the already broken front windshield. A hard crack. One. Then another. Another.

The crazy sonofabitch is using a crowbar!

"I know you're not dead yet, you bastard," Jesse snarled. "But you will be when I'm done with you!"

Okay, screw this shit. Wyatt stretched for the glove box. His legs were still freaking trapped, but he could get to a weapon. He'd put his gun in that glove box earlier, before they'd gone to Forth's place. Just in case. Just because he'd been in high vigilance mode with Christy.

The crowbar slammed down again. "I will *break you* into pieces!" Jesse yelled.

Yep, clearly, they'd found her stalker. Or maybe both brothers were just insane. They'd work out the details later. Later as in...*after* Wyatt stopped the psycho from killing him.

He yanked open the glove box.

And Jesse drove the crowbar into the driver's side window.

Glass rained in on Wyatt.

***

"It's not like the night with our parents." Forth leaned forward as he stared out of the windshield. "It's not like that night. Do you hear me, Christy? Wyatt is going to be all right. He'll be fine. Fine."

Christy's hands had a death grip on the steering wheel. Forth's car. She'd grabbed the keys and rushed out and been behind the driver's seat in a blink. Not about to be left behind, Forth had jumped in the passenger seat. He'd called the cops while she drove.

And now...*Where are you, Wyatt? Where?*

She couldn't think about the night with her parents. A night that had been too much like this one. Icy roads. Too much darkness. The night a deer—a scared deer—had rushed across the road and her father had jerked the wheel instinctively.

But Mountain Brook had its name for a reason. The roads were up high. They twisted. They turned and...

We went off the road. Tumbled down, down, down. She could hear the screech of metal. The screams from her parents and...

Her parents had been dead on impact.

She'd drifted in and out of consciousness.

A deer. A scared deer.

Everything had been gone in a blink. Everything.

"Christy, it's *not* like that night."

Ice covered her body. "I can't lose him."

"*We* aren't losing him. We're finding him. I'm telling him I'm sorry for being an asshole. I'm gonna let him take two punches at me. Then you're gonna tell him you love him, and we are going home for Christmas and—*car! There!*"

She hit the brakes. The vehicle started to slide, and terror clawed at her. *Not again. Not again. Not—*

The car stopped.

"Jesus!" Forth's hands slammed into the dash. "*Jesus.*"

She looked through the windshield. Her headlights had hit another vehicle, a dark Range

Rover. The front end was smashed. Chunks of glass were all over the road.

Broken.

"That's not Wyatt's ride," Forth said, his voice a mix of both worry and relief. "He doesn't have a Range Rover—"

"That's the vehicle Jesse was driving." She'd seen it at Forth's house. A black Range Rover. Her shaking hands shoved open her door. "*Wyatt!*" Christy screamed. Her booted feet ran over the broken glass.

Jesse's ride was right at the side of the road. But she could tell—from the twisted, broken pines—that another car had gone over the edge. Off the road and *over the edge*.

"*Wyatt!*" she screamed again as her whole world seemed to implode.

***

He couldn't quite reach *inside* the glove box. Wyatt's fingers strained. His arm strained. His shoulder.

"Got you, you bastard!" Jesse shouted. More glass rained down from the driver's side.

Whatever the hell had gone into Wyatt's chest—part of the gear shift?—Wyatt knew he had no choice. It was locking him in place, and he had to wrench it aside so he could stretch a few more inches. But as soon as he did...

Blood poured from the wound.

And pain blasted through him.

But he could reach into that glove box now.

Jesse laughed. "Gonna drive this crowbar into your—"

"Wyatt!"

Jesse jerked back. With the crowbar.

"Wyatt!" Christy's scream came again. "Where are you? *Wyatt?"*

"No!" A snarl from Jesse. "She can't be here. She can't get to you. She *won't."* And he whirled away.

He was going...after Christy? With the crowbar? "Come...back!" Wyatt yelled. Only his voice came out strained. "Come back...for me...you..." He stretched more and grabbed the gun that he'd put inside the glove box earlier. He turned back to his door. Shoved it.

But the damn thing wouldn't open.

And his legs were still fucking trapped.

"No!" From Wyatt. Louder. More desperate. Because that bastard had been going after Christy with a crowbar. "Come back!"

"Wyatt?" Christy's frantic voice. Close. So close.

But where did Jesse go? Jesse...and his crowbar.

Wyatt kicked and shoved against the material pinning his feet and calves. *Fuck me. I think my left ankle is broken.* Wonderful. "Get out of here!" he roared to Christy. Tried to roar. "Run, call the..." His breath heaved. "Cops! Call...cops!"

Hands slapped into the side of his vehicle.

Wyatt flinched.

But it was Christy.

"Wyatt! I was so worried!"

"Get...away."

"I'm getting you help." She tried opening the door and swore in frustration when it remained stuck. Then Christy tilted the light from her phone into the SUV so she could see him. "Forth is right behind me. We are going to get you out of here. There's so much blood...oh, Wyatt..."

Someone was behind her. He could see the movement. The shadowy form. But...he didn't think it was Forth. "Go..."

"There is no way I'm leaving you. I love you. Do you hear me? I love you. I was going to tell you that later, in a way more romantic setting, but you need to know. Right here. Right now. You're it for me. There will never be anyone else. I love you—"

A guttural scream broke through her words. And Wyatt knew he'd been right. That wasn't Forth behind her. For all Wyatt knew, Jesse had already taken out his best friend. And now that shadowy form was charging for Christy. Wyatt was trapped. And Christy—

She'd just spun around and the light from her phone hit Jesse's charging form. He had the crowbar up and was getting ready to swing it.

Christy ducked. The crowbar slammed into the side of the already broken vehicle.

And Wyatt fired the gun he'd taken from the glove box. The powerful boom filled the car, even as Jesse wrenched back, like a puppet pulled by a string.

Wyatt fired a second time.

Another hit.

The crowbar fell from Jesse's fingers. He stumbled.

Then Forth erupted from the darkness and tackled him. Forth took the bastard down to the ground even as Christy rushed forward with her light and grabbed the crowbar.

"This jackass hit me from behind!" Forth shouted. "I swear, he knocked me out for a few seconds. Sonofabitch!"

Christy brought the crowbar back to the SUV. And she started trying to open the door. "I'm getting you out," she told Wyatt. "You're getting out, you're coming back with me, you're going to be all right..."

Blood had soaked his shirt. "Nothing vital...hurt..."

"You'd better not be lying to me."

He...sort of was. He had no idea how extensive the damage was. He just didn't want her worrying. "Love...you..."

A siren wailed in the distance.

"Forth!" Christy yelled. *"Help me!"*

Wyatt's head bumped against what he thought was the steering wheel. The wheel and maybe a deflated air bag. Dammit. He *might* be worse than he'd realized...Blood pumped from his chest, and his vision had started going dark. Extra dark.

But at least the bad guy was out of commission. At least Christy was safe. At least...

"I love you!" she yelled at him.

At least the woman of his dreams loved him.

"Don't you *dare* die on me!" The crowbar jammed into the side of the vehicle. "Don't you dare! You're going to love me for fifty years! We're going to have a house full of kids, and we are going to be stupid, ridiculously happy! You aren't dying! You aren't—"

His eyes drifted closed, but he still managed to tell her, "Wouldn't...dream of it." No, his dreams didn't involve dying.

His dreams involved her. The next fifty years. The house full of kids...

Love.

"Forth, help me!" she bellowed.

"I was subduing the bad guy—shit, I'm...*Wyatt? Wyatt, look at me! Look at me!*"

But his eyes just didn't want to open.

"Christy, it's not like last time," Forth said. Wyatt heard his voice so clearly. "He's not going to die. He's not. *We won't let him.*"

That wasn't quite the way that medicine worked. Not about *letting* things. And Wyatt would tell his buddy that but...

But he was past the point of saying anything.

CHAPTER ELEVEN

"I am so sorry."

Wyatt cracked open one eye.

Forth appeared miserable as he slouched near the hospital bed. "I should never, ever have hit you." His eyes were on the floor.

"You...can't hit for shit."

Forth's eyes whipped up toward Wyatt. A wide smile curved his lips.

But before Forth could speak again, the hospital room door flew open. Wyatt turned his head, fully expecting to see Christy rushing to his bedside.

It wasn't Christy.

It was a Christmas-scrub-wearing Axel.

"Well, well, well..." Axel smirked at him. "Guess who decided to finally wake up?"

Wyatt licked his dry lips. "Christy..."

"No, I'm Axel." Axel leaned forward and checked Wyatt's vitals. "And if you're getting us confused, then I need to worry about head injuries."

Wyatt swatted him away. "Christy. Where...is she?" His throat felt scratchy. But at least there was no tube stopping him from speaking. *Maybe there was one in my throat earlier?* He should probably ask about his injuries. He would. Later. When he wasn't so worried about Christy.

"She's taking care of a small errand. Don't worry. She was at your side every moment. Even when I told her you were utterly fine. A broken ankle. Pretty deep laceration to the chest. But nothing you won't heal from. Hell, you can even go home tomorrow morning. You can spend Christmas all snug and happy." Axel flashed a light in Wyatt's eyes. "Aren't you the lucky one?"

Christy was okay. Yes, he felt very, very lucky. "Jesse?"

"He's locked up," Forth hurried to tell him. "Guy is crazy, by the way."

I noticed.

"Ramone wasn't the real stalker. It was Jesse."

Figured that one out for myself.

"Ramone was following orders from Jesse all along. The guy seems terrified of Jesse. So scared he was willing to go to jail for him." Forth paused. "Probably so scared because Jesse is a freaking psycho who tried to kill you."

"A psycho who *won't* be going near your girl again," Axel assured Wyatt. "Not with all the charges against him. And, by the way, two bullets had to be dug out of the fellow. You weren't in the mood to screw around, huh?"

Hell, no. It had been life or death. "He was...going after Christy."

"He won't ever be doing that again." Axel nodded. "Guess you had to play the hero even when you were pinned in the car, huh?"

He hadn't been playing anything. Christy had been in danger. Protecting her had been the only option.

The door opened again. This time, finally, Christy stood on the threshold. She had one hand tucked behind her back. Faint holiday music drifted from that open doorway.

When she saw that Wyatt was awake, a relieved smile spread over her face. Her dimple winked at him. "Hi."

"Hi," he told her. The tension in his chest eased. Everything suddenly seemed fine. No, a whole lot better than fine.

Perfect.

Forth cleared his throat. "I, um, I'm supposed to apologize. Formally and deeply."

Wyatt didn't take his gaze off Christy.

"I'm sorry that I'm a dick." Forth coughed. "Christy said I had to use those exact words. I'm sorry, and I hope you know, man, how much I love you."

Okay, now Wyatt did peer over at Forth.

"You're my best friend," Forth said simply. Gruffly. "And my sister is lucky to be with a guy like you." A long breath. "All right, now, I'm heading out. Because...I know she has something to say to you." He grabbed Axel and they left...even as Christy made her way to the hospital bed.

She still had one hand behind her back.

"Hi," she said once more.

He just drank her in.

"Do you remember what I said to you...at the accident scene?"

He remembered bits and pieces. Mostly, he remembered being scared that she would be hurt.

"Wasn't certain you'd remember, so I wanted to make sure and say everything again." She took a deep breath. "Wyatt Roth, I love you."

He blinked.

"I think I might have been in love with you for years. No other guy ever felt *right* for me, because I already knew my Mr. Right. It's you." She bit her lower lip, then said, "I love you. And I would really, really like for us to give this thing between us a chance."

"This...thing?"

"I want to be with you." Soft. "I want to love you. I want—"

"Fifty years," he remembered. "A house full of kids."

Her eyes filled with tears, but Christy blinked them away.

"I want that," he told her. "I want you." She was all he'd ever wanted. He'd been waiting for her. Did she realize that?

A tear slid down her cheek. One she hadn't been able to blink away. And she lifted her hand from behind her back. He realized she held mistletoe—mistletoe that dangled from a small, red ribbon.

"I borrowed this from Naya," she admitted. "Because this is kinda how we started. With a kiss. Only when I first thought about getting under the mistletoe with you, I wasn't brave enough to say...I want to kiss you, Wyatt. I want to kiss you and love you and have a life with you."

He wanted *all* of that. Everything.

She leaned over him. Lifted the mistletoe over their heads.

Then she brought her mouth to his.

And kissed him.

I want to kiss you and love you and have a life with you.

Hell, yes.

Best Christmas *ever*.

Despite the fact that he was spread out in a hospital bed...

Best. Christmas. Ever.

***

Wyatt unlocked the door to his house. He had to move gingerly because a cast covered his left foot and ankle and curved up his calf. So maybe his walk was a little lurchy, but he had one arm around Christy's shoulders, she smelled like the most delicious strawberries in the world, and he wasn't about to complain about a damn thing.

She's safe. The bad guy—correction, the bad guys are in jail. Now I get to spend Christmas with the woman I love.

Christy shut the door behind them. "Forth is coming over later. He wants to make dinner for you. It's part of his apology tour."

A tour that had been going non-stop. And it was great that Forth wanted to come over. Wonderful. But Wyatt had rather hoped to make a meal out of Christy by kissing and savoring every single inch of her.

But Forth wouldn't stay forever.

As soon as he leaves, she's mine.

No, she already was his. Finally.

"Can you, ah, stay here, for just a moment?" She slipped from beneath his hold. "Seriously, just count and give me like sixty seconds."

Before he could respond, she'd darted toward the den.

Wyatt frowned after her. Then he realized he was supposed to be counting. Only he didn't actually count. He frowned more.

"Ready!" Christy called out. "In the den!"

He lurched toward the den. Paused to glare at his foot. Then lurched some more. His head lifted up as he neared—

"Surprise," Christy announced as she stood in the middle of his den.

The Christmas tree glowed behind her. *Glowed.* His sad strands of lights weren't the only things on the tree any longer. She'd decked it out completely. Gorgeous ornaments. Bright, curling ribbons. She'd strung lights all over the room. Stockings hung near the chimney. Wrapped presents waited under the tree.

"I wanted it to look happy and festive when you came home." Her hands twisted in front of her. "When I pulled out your decorations, I realized you still had all the glass ornaments I'd made for you over the years. Even the first one that I made when I was just sixteen."

His gaze darted to the tree. Unerringly, he found that gorgeous red ball of blown glass. The one she'd made at her very first glassblowing class and given to him. "Red is your favorite color," he heard himself say.

"You kept them all...because..."

"Because you made them. Because I love you." Simple.

She stopped twisting her hands. She flew across the room and into his arms. Just the way he'd always imagined her doing. *Running to me.*

"I love you." Christy squeezed him tight.

He didn't mind the stab of pain that came from his stitches. If one popped, he'd just sew himself back up.

Over her shoulder, he looked at the tree. At all the ornaments that had been so carefully hung. The stockings. He hadn't actually *owned* stockings. She must have bought them when he'd been at the hospital.

One for him.

One for her.

Hung like they were a family.

Because we are.

"What do you think?" Christy asked him. "Is the tree okay?"

"Beautiful," Wyatt replied. But he wasn't talking about the tree.

Christy eased back and stared up at him.

"Beautiful," he said again because she was.

And there wasn't any mistletoe around, but who cared? He bent his head and kissed her.

I finally have my Christmas wish.

THE END

A NOTE FROM THE AUTHOR

I love the holiday season. To be honest with you, I usually start decking my halls in early November. I try to savor every drop of joy that I can at Christmas. I love singing carols, I love watching Christmas movies, and I absolutely adore reading Christmas romance books.

I hope you had a fun time reading Wyatt and Christy's story. My goal was to just make readers smile and feel a little happier during the holidays.

If you'd like to stay updated on my releases and sales, please join my newsletter list.

https://cynthiaeden.com/newsletter/

May your holiday season be merry, bright, and filled with delight.

Best,
Cynthia Eden
cynthiaeden.com

ABOUT THE AUTHOR

Cynthia Eden is a *New York Times*, *USA Today*, *Digital Book World*, and *IndieReader* bestselling author of romantic suspense and paranormal romance. She's a prolific author who lives along the Alabama Gulf Coast. In her free time, you'll find her reading romances, watching horror movies, or hunting for adventures. She's a chocolate addict and a major *Supernatural* fan.

For More Information

- *cynthiaeden.com*
- *facebook.com/cynthiaedenfanpage*

HER OTHER WORKS

Ice Breaker Cold Case Romance

- Frozen In Ice (Book 1)
- Falling For The Ice Queen (Book 2)
- Ice Cold Saint (Book 3)
- Touched By Ice (Book 4)
- Trapped In Ice (Book 5)
- Forged From Ice (Book 6)
- Buried Under Ice (Book 7)

Wilde Ways

- Protecting Piper (Book 1)
- Guarding Gwen (Book 2)
- Before Ben (Book 3)
- The Heart You Break (Book 4)
- Fighting For Her (Book 5)
- Ghost Of A Chance (Book 6)
- Crossing The Line (Book 7)
- Counting On Cole (Book 8)
- Chase After Me (Book 9)
- Say I Do (Book 10)
- Roman Will Fall (Book 11)
- The One Who Got Away (Book 12)
- Pretend You Want Me (Book 13)
- Cross My Heart (Book 14)
- The Bodyguard Next Door (Book 15)

- Ex Marks The Perfect Spot (Book 16)
- The Thief Who Loved Me (Book 17)

Wilde Ways: Gone Rogue

- How To Protect A Princess (Book 1)
- How To Heal A Heartbreak (Book 2)
- How To Con A Crime Boss (Book 3)

Trouble For Hire

- No Escape From War (Book 1)
- Don't Play With Odin (Book 2)
- Jinx, You're It (Book 3)
- Remember Ramsey (Book 4)

Death and Moonlight Mystery

- Step Into My Web (Book 1)
- Save Me From The Dark (Book 2)

Phoenix Fury

- Hot Enough To Burn (Book 1)
- Slow Burn (Book 2)
- Burn It Down (Book 3)

Dark Sins

- Don't Trust A Killer (Book 1)
- Don't Love A Liar (Book 2)

Lazarus Rising

- Never Let Go (Book One)
- Keep Me Close (Book Two)
- Stay With Me (Book Three)
- Run To Me (Book Four)
- Lie Close To Me (Book Five)
- Hold On Tight (Book Six)

Bad Things

- The Devil In Disguise (Book 1)
- On The Prowl (Book 2)
- Undead Or Alive (Book 3)
- Broken Angel (Book 4)
- Heart Of Stone (Book 5)
- Tempted By Fate (Book 6)
- Wicked And Wild (Book 7)
- Saint Or Sinner (Book 8)

Bite Series

- Forbidden Bite (Bite Book 1)
- Mating Bite (Bite Book 2)

Blood and Moonlight Series

- Bite The Dust (Book 1)
- Better Off Undead (Book 2)
- Bitter Blood (Book 3)

Mine Series

- Mine To Take (Book 1)
- Mine To Keep (Book 2)
- Mine To Hold (Book 3)
- Mine To Crave (Book 4)
- Mine To Have (Book 5)
- Mine To Protect (Book 6)

Dark Obsession Series

- Watch Me (Book 1)
- Want Me (Book 2)
- Need Me (Book 3)
- Beware Of Me (Book 4)
- Only For Me (Books 1 to 4)

Purgatory Series

- The Wolf Within (Book 1)
- Marked By The Vampire (Book 2)
- Charming The Beast (Book 3)
- Deal with the Devil (Book 4)
- The Beasts Inside (Books 1 to 4)

Bound Series

- Bound By Blood (Book 1)
- Bound In Darkness (Book 2)
- Bound In Sin (Book 3)
- Bound By The Night (Book 4)
- Bound in Death (Book 5)
- Forever Bound (Books 1 to 4)

Stand-Alone Romantic Suspense

- Waiting For Christmas
- Monster Without Mercy
- Kiss Me This Christmas
- It's A Wonderful Werewolf
- Never Cry Werewolf
- Immortal Danger
- Deck The Halls
- Come Back To Me
- Put A Spell On Me
- Never Gonna Happen
- One Hot Holiday
- Slay All Day
- Midnight Bite
- Secret Admirer
- Christmas With A Spy
- Femme Fatale
- Until Death
- Sinful Secrets

- **First Taste of Darkness**
- **A Vampire's Christmas Carol**